WAKING UP ON MOON DOG DAY

# WAKING UP ON MOON DOG DAY

by

Jon McKenney

SLYJACK BOOKS

Library of Congress Control Number 2018904263
ISBN 978-0-9889613-1-9




Publisher's Cataloging-in-Publication Data
McKenney, Jon
Waking up on moon dog day / Jon McKenney
ISBN 978-0-9889613-1-9

Cover Art: Théodore Rousseau, *Marshy Landscape* (1842)

Book Design by the Frogtown Bookmaker
frogtownbookmaker.com

Published by SLYJACK BOOKS

For Beth Tashery Shannon

# HOT DAY IN SEAMY RAW WISHES

So then afterwards, when I finally had a quiet moment, I glanced through that article, the one entitled "How Do You Know You're Not Dreaming?" I learned in the first paragraph that pinching yourself is not the answer, but I never got to the answer (if there was one), because just then someone began pounding on the door of my apartment.

I opened to a little man standing there holding a package. He couldn't have been much over four feet and he was nearly as wide as he was tall and he had no neck. He wore the dull green uniform of his delivery service, his company's name stitched across a shirt pocket, but I forget what the name was. Two short stubs of arms held the package, which was half as big as he was and cylindrical like a hatbox and wrapped in thin, white wrapping paper. It was loosely bound in dark twine with a decorative red bow uncurling on top. The address label bore the word OCCUPANT and nothing else. I didn't see a return address.

"Who's it from?" I said.

"I only deliver them, I don't ship them."

"It's not addressed to me."

"You're the occupant, aren't you?"

"I'm *an* occupant, I'm not the *only* occupant in the building."

"It's not addressed to *only* occupant in the building, it's just addressed to occupant."

Hardly bending over, he set the package at my feet and flourished a clipboard he pulled out from under his arm.

"Sign here," he said.

"I'm not signing for that."

"Fine."

He took out a red marking pen and wrote REFUSED on the package, then he wrote REFUSED on the clipboard and started to walk away.

"What are you doing?" I said. "Don't leave it here."

"Why not? You refused it."

"So take it back."

"I just deliver incoming, I don't do outgoing." He headed toward the street door.

"Wait," I said. He stopped and turned around. It was a nimble movement, and I'm not sure how he did it. Maybe he spun around on one heel, or maybe he jumped up half an inch or so and turned in the air, but it happened so fast I couldn't really see it happening.

"How do you know you're not dreaming?" I said. That was the only parting shot I could come up with — the title of the article I was about to read when he pounded on my door. An edge of his upper lip curled back, showing a long, yellow, tusk-like tooth.

"That's the dumbest question I heard all day," he said and turned away with the same nimble movement.

He waddled out toward the street and I picked up the package and took it inside and closed the door with my foot. The package was heavy. The little man must've been very strong despite his size. The knot holding it together was coming undone and I wasn't sure I should open the package, so I set it on the dining room table and put my right forefinger on the knot. The knot was a small, thready tangle, somewhat slimy, and the loose ends began curling around my finger and formed a bow that, with no help from me, suddenly tightened around the finger.

The finger began to turn purple. I wiggled it to shake it loose from the bowknot, but the bowknot held tight. The white wrapping paper was thin tissue. It whispered like a breeze in dry grass when I wiggled my finger. The box was heavy and I couldn't guess what was in it and nothing inside rattled, ticked or moved around when I shook it. After a while my fingernail turned black, came loose and fell off.

I didn't feel any pain when it came off, I felt nothing, not even a phantom pain where the fingernail had been. With my free hand I opened a medical encyclopedia and looked up my symptoms. It said I had digital necrosis, indexical variety, a common affliction, but not to worry, the prognosis was excellent, and I should avoid pointing, tapping, typing, drumming, playing a musical instrument, or picking my nose with the affected finger.

After a while the decorative red bow came loose and the knot of dark twine released my finger. By now my fingertip had swollen to three or four times its normal size. It looked like a fleshy bulb and for a moment I imagined that's where my hand came from, like a pale, uprooted plant sprouting from the same finger-bulb year after year. But that didn't seem very plausible. Maybe it didn't do that. I'm just guessing.

I picked up the hatbox with both hands and shook it. It seemed to have grown heavier. If it was a hatbox it must've contained a heavy hat, maybe a medieval jouster's helmet. I didn't want to open it, not after all the trouble it gave me. And I was suddenly unsure if I even had the right to open it.

I thought about that for a long time. What gives you the right to open things?

Thinking about it gave me a headache. I looked up my headache symptoms in the medical encyclopedia, but I couldn't find any that matched. There were all types of headaches listed, but none of them were headaches caused by thinking about something for a long time. Then I thought maybe my headache didn't really exist. But how could that be, when I felt it there, gushing behind my eyes? Well, pains exist when you feel them. If you don't feel them then they don't exist. There's no such thing as an illusory pain. Even a phantom pain is a real pain, not an illusionary pain. Like all ghosts it has just lost its way and doesn't know where it belongs. You hurt, therefore you are. I don't know where that thought came from. It doesn't sound like something I would think of. It just sounds like one more thing to make everything hurt more.

Anyway, the medical encyclopedia and the hatbox (if that's what it was) were more likely to be illusory than the pain. So I threw the medical encyclopedia across the room. Trying to put its unreality to the test, I guess. It made a dent in the wall, which spit out a bit of plaster dust where the book struck. The book made a cracking sound when it struck, and I knew its back was broken. It writhed a moment on the floor beside the wall, flipping its pages as if in agony, and then lay still. A real drama queen, that book. Which all seemed pretty real to me, strange as it was.

I wanted to throw the hatbox, too (if hatbox it was), but then I thought the rightful owner, whoever OCCUPANT was, would be pissed if he, or maybe she, came to reclaim it. That is, if I wasn't the owner, a question I was much in doubt about. And which my thinking about had given me a headache, among all the other headaches I had.

But how could I have other headaches all at the same time? Wasn't it just one big headache, or was it a congregation of little headaches?

Then I thought that though pains can't be illusory, the causes of pains can be, and that the cause of this headache, or these headaches, was my thinking too long about the ownership of the hatbox (if that's what it really was). So it was my thinking about it that was illusory, even though the headache wasn't, or the headaches weren't. But how could that be, when I felt the thoughts trickling behind my eyes? And thoughts, like pains, if you feel them, can't be illusory. And if you can't feel them, how can you have them?

The room was getting stuffy from all those thoughts and headaches, or headache if there was only one, and I needed to get some air. The street outside was silent, wind-swept, full of fitful sunshine, full of more air than I could breathe all at once. It was a little past noon, which I thought was strange, because the last time I looked I had thought it was closer to sundown, and that couldn't have been too long ago.

Shadows faded away and reappeared in bold outline on the pavement. The street seemed strangely still and all in motion at the same time. I thought a short walk would help clear my head, and I set off down the street. Or maybe it was up the street.

A one-armed man sat on the curb, his feet in the gutter. He was looking down between his splayed legs. He looked up as I approached and he nodded as if in recognition. His face seemed familiar but I couldn't place it. I wondered if he knew me or if I had once known him and had forgotten that I knew him. Or whether he nodded just to be sociable.

Then his head drooped as I passed, and I wondered if I should've nodded in return or said something. I almost stopped to ask him if that's what I should've done. But now he seemed so interested in the ground between his feet that I didn't want to interrupt whatever pleasure it gave him, if pleasure is what made him look down like that. I didn't want to interrupt his silence, even if it gave him no pleasure at all. It seemed like an invasion of privacy to intrude in a thoughtful man's thoughts, no matter how many headaches they were giving him and no matter how publicly he was having them.

As I passed on I thought that I should've said something to the man. That thought began to weigh heavily on me. The weight of it became painful, like the weight of the hatbox (if it was a hatbox) dangling from my finger. I carried too much pain already from my other thoughts and I suddenly decided to get rid of this thought once for all, and turned around to go back to the man. I didn't know what I was going to say to him, but I was pretty sure the idea would come to me before I got within speaking distance.

But the street was empty. The man was no longer sitting on the curb looking down between his splayed legs. I stood there a moment, annoyed by this lost opportunity to speak to him. Relieved, too, that I no longer had to speak to him.

But then I thought maybe I did have to speak to him, even though he was no longer there to be spoken to. In fact, what in the world made me think his absence relieved me of the responsibility to speak to him? What a jackass I was to think I could wriggle out from under the obligation. Like my finger wriggling out from under that bowknot.

But then I wasn't quite sure that I did have an obligation, jackass or not. I'm pretty sure I could be a jackass in any case, no matter my obligation. I don't know how I knew that. The idea just came to me, I guess. Anyway, I decided to speak to the next person I met and just say the first thing that came into my head. What that might be I couldn't even guess, since the only things in my head were my worries about the hatbox (if that's what it was), and my obligation to speak to the man sitting on the curb (I mean, if I had an obligation), and of course the pains that were filling my head because of the thoughts that had already filled it.

And soon a young woman came walking briskly toward me. She had puffy, blond hair that bounced as she walked along. She was wearing a tweedy brown jacket and carried a large beige purse tucked under her left arm. And suddenly I knew what I was going to say. But she must've seen something in the way I angled my body at her, since she turned her head away and looked out at the street just when I was about to speak.

"Excuse me — " I started. Not a bad way to start, but I felt strangely humiliated doing it. I guess I wasn't used to excusing myself. "Do you mind if I..." But she kept on walking, her head turned away from me. From the tiny quiver of her head, I'm pretty sure she heard me, and I felt like following her till I had finished saying what I was about to say to her, plus a few nasty comments which I hadn't been about to say till I saw that tiny quiver of her head.

But probably she would've started yelling for the cops and I was still feeling too polite to break in on someone's privacy like that, even when they were indulging it in public, where you'd think whatever they're doing should be a matter of common ownership. But I let her get away and looked around for someone else.

Down the street, or maybe up it, an older woman, and shabbier, was pulling a two-wheeled wire shopping cart. Occasionally pausing, she hoisted to her lips a bottle in a brown paper bag, and drank.

"How do you know you're not dreaming?" I asked quickly, before she could get away. Not that she could, since she moved slowly and dragged a heavy burden in her wire shopping cart. She seemed unsurprised at my question, even pleased that I had asked her.

"I don't know how I know," she said. "But I know I am." Then she said softly, maybe as an afterthought: "I hope I wake up soon." She shuffled off, dragging her wire shopping cart.

Two young men came along. They looked like students. But maybe they weren't. Now that I think about it, I'm no longer sure what someone has to look like to look like a student. They didn't even look all that young. Or sometimes they did, but then a moment later they looked older. Or one of them looked older and the other younger. Then they would switch off, looking alternately younger and older by the moment. But definitely one was taller than the other. For some reason their heights didn't change from one moment to the next even while their ages kept changing, otherwise I wouldn't have known whom to speak to.

The taller one seemed annoyed by my question and wanted to hurry on. But the shorter one was amused and seemed to give it some thought. After a moment, while his companion grumbled quietly, the shorter one said, "If you think you're dreaming you're not dreaming, because if you're dreaming you're not thinking, and if you're not thinking you can't know anything."

The two ambled off, the shorter one repeating his answer several times and laughing, pleased with himself, while his companion grimaced and grumbled. I thought if he was right, and I was dreaming, then all those thoughts that had given me a headache weren't thoughts at all. But then what had given me the headache? I'm pretty sure it was those thoughts. In fact, thinking about those thoughts now was giving me another headache, and if I was really thinking about them then I couldn't be dreaming, according to the shorter student, if that's what he really was. So either he was wrong, or I was wide awake. A moment later I stopped a fidgety little man, who seemed terrified of the question.

"What do you mean?" he said. Which I thought was a good question, maybe better than the one I had asked. But before I could tell him this, he scurried away, making a wide semi-circle around me, so I turned to a large woman in a bright, blue pants suit.

"Whatever happened to your hand?" said the large woman in the bright, blue pants suit, ignoring my question. "You need to get that looked at," she said and reached out as if to grab the hand. When I drew it back she twisted her mouth and made a sucking noise with her tongue and hurried on.

Then I asked a shaggy man, who reeked of last month's garbage, who said, "Fuck you."

I wondered if I should punch him in the face. But my punching hand was my right hand, and I wasn't sure my right forefinger was up to it. Then I realized he wasn't talking to me. He was responding to someone in his mind, maybe himself. Maybe whoever was in his mind was giving him headaches, too, and I suddenly felt sympathetic. And when he realized I had just asked him a question, he looked confused and abashed, so I left him alone.

By then I was getting tired of asking the same question over and over, and I walked past a lot of people without speaking to them. And then I recalled what the woman in the bright, blue pants suit had said, and all the pains in my head came back in a rush, despite all the fresh air I had inhaled since leaving home.

I raised my right hand and looked at my forefinger, which by now had swollen to five or six times its normal size. "This is one hand," I said aloud, and then raised the left hand and looked at it. "And this is another." Somehow that trivial reminder felt reassuring. And just then the forefinger fell off my right hand.

It bounced along the pavement like a rubber ball, or maybe it had grown little legs and actually hopped along the pavement. I wasn't sure, it moved so fast, and disappeared down a sewer drain. I stared at the gap between my thumb and middle finger. Necrosis had already begun to invade the palm. It didn't hurt, in fact I couldn't feel anything. I leaned my face into a brick wall so that nobody would see me weeping over the loss of a stupid forefinger, or maybe just to pound my head against the bricks a little, and then I decided I'd had enough fresh air and started home.

I passed familiar landmarks, but after a couple of blocks they stopped being familiar. I retraced my steps, but what I turned back to seemed not so familiar as the landmarks I had just passed. Not even my right hand looked familiar. My right hand had once been the most familiar landmark of my body. Whatever resemblance the two hands had once shared had disappeared. That right-handed four-fingered monstrosity looked nothing like a hand, so how could I be so sure about the other, even though it looked normal? Or at least I thought it looked normal. I held up the left hand and said, "Are you normal?" Not that I expected an answer. How could the stupid thing respond to a childish question like that, even if it could answer?

But the more I looked at it the less certain I was whether it was normal. Maybe the right hand was normal, and the left hand the monstrosity. And now even the left hand no longer looked familiar. Only the fitful sunlight and the shadows that faded away and reappeared in bold outlines, only these were familiar, and yet these were the only things that kept changing.

The street seemed to stretch forever past low buildings I no longer recognized. Both ends of the street stretched into a distant haze. I was hoping to see the man who sat on the curb, staring down between his legs, since I knew he was just a short distance from my apartment building. Remembering his cordial nod as I passed, I suddenly decided I liked the man. As for all the unfamiliar things around me, I felt more angry than afraid.

I would've pressed my head against a brick wall again, but there were no longer any brick walls in sight. All the store fronts were dark glass windows that I could barely see through. I thought I saw dim shapes moving behind the glass but I wasn't sure. I would've pressed my face against the glass but I didn't want people inside looking out at me with my face like that. That is, if there were people inside. Maybe there weren't and I just imagined them.

If I had known there weren't any people inside I would've gone ahead and pressed my face against the glass and wept again, or maybe beat my head against the glass. Not that crying or beating my head ever helped. Not that I had anything to cry over or to beat my head about, come to think of it. Except losing my finger, but so what? I still had a bunch left. And getting lost, which maybe wasn't really something to fuss about.

In fact, come to think of it, I had hardly felt anything at all when I was fussing about them. Maybe all that fresh air had cleared out my headaches, and now I was trying to feel something just because I thought I should, in case there was something worth fussing about, even though maybe there wasn't.

I would've peeked through the doors to find out if there were people inside, but the doors must've been in the rear of the buildings, and I couldn't find any passageways to the rear. What an unusual way to do business, I thought. Stores without doors. They must cater to a very special clientele. I was obviously not one of their customers, or if I had once been a customer I had completely forgotten by now. So I continued on up, or maybe down, the street.

I came to a news rack. It was a clear plastic box mounted on spindly metal legs chained to a sign post. The sign on the sign post said: NO PARKING BETWEEN THE H, and someone had spray painted over the rest of it. If H meant hours (followed by the times no parking was permitted between), then those hours must've been right now, because I didn't see any cars parked anywhere on the street. The clear plastic box wasn't so clear either. Someone had spray painted over most of it, too.

A stack of newspapers sat inside but I saw only part of a headline, HOT DAY IN SEA. I wondered if that was some kind of weather report. But then it should have been *at* sea, not *in* sea.Or maybe it was saying the day was hot underwater, or maybe it was saying something about the season and the rest of the word "season" had disappeared behind a cloud of gray paint.

I tried to open the box but it was stuck. Then I realized I needed to drop four quarters in the slot. The earth had four quarters and so did the moon, but I had none. I don't know where that thought came from. It doesn't sound like something I would think.

Sometimes people dropped quarters in the street. Any dropped quarters on the sidewalk would have been scooped up already. But maybe there were some in the gutter that had been overlooked, so I walked along the edge of the sidewalk, looking for quarters in the gutter. I wondered how I had become streetwise so quickly. I almost felt smug about it. But I didn't find any quarters, and maybe I wasn't so streetwise after all. I began to think I'd never find out what it meant for days to be hot *in* sea, or *at* sea, or underwater, or seasonally, or whatever those days were supposed to be. Somehow it suddenly seemed important to find out what they were.

Then I thought, You should just smash open the box. The same fear came over me as I had felt about the hatbox (if that's what it was) with the sticky, black twine tied around it. What right did I have to open this box, or that one, or any box? But this was no time to worry about who had the right. I looked back at the news rack, almost afraid it had disappeared along with all the other familiar things. But it was still there. In fact I was standing right next to it. I wondered how that could be, since I thought I had walked a long time looking for quarters. Maybe I had only dreamed I was walking. But how could that be, when I was wide awake? Or if I wasn't, then smashing open the box should wake me up, so I smashed it open.

There wasn't anything inside. Someone must've taken the newspapers when I had turned my back, even while I was standing right next to it. Then I thought, Of course! This must be a different news rack, even though it looks exactly like the first news rack I saw, or looked exactly like it before I smashed it. And I had drubbed it pretty thoroughly, probably more than it needed for me to open it. In fact, I had smashed the clear plastic box almost flat. I must've been stronger than I thought, or angrier. I almost felt proud of myself.

But I had hurt what was left of my right hand. The knuckles were bleeding and the third and fourth fingers were twisted like corkscrews. It didn't matter. Necrosis was creeping up the third and fourth fingers, and I couldn't feel anything there. I continued on down the street, looking for another news rack.

Or maybe I continued on up the street. The street was flat, so I couldn't tell if I was going up or down it. Then I thought to check my shadow. It was a little past noon, I thought, so the sun was veering westward, and my shadow should've tended to my left if I was heading south, or to my right if north, or in front of me if east, or in back of me if west. On a map, south is usually at the bottom of the page, which is why we call south "down", and north at the top of the page is "up", so I should've been able to tell, even on a flat street, just by looking at my shadow, whether I was going down or going up, or going out west, or going back east. Don't ask why east is "back" and west is "out". I was having enough trouble telling up from down.

In any case, I couldn't really tell which way my shadow tended. Sometimes it seemed to go one way, and then a cloud would pass over, and after that my shadow would reappear going the other way. Maybe I was walking in circles and didn't even know it. To check my shadow again, I decided to wait till the sky cleared, then I would find out.

I came to another news rack, but this one had been smashed almost as badly as the one I had just smashed, and it was empty. After that I passed dozens of smashed and empty news racks, and I got so used to seeing them that I stopped looking for them, and so I stopped seeing them. Finally I passed a restaurant and realized I was hungry. Unlike the other shops, this restaurant had clear glass windows and I saw customers inside and waitresses scurrying around bringing plates of food and carrying off empty ones. I looked around for the door but like the other shops the restaurant didn't have one.

I rapped on the window to get someone's attention and a bald man sitting alone near the window looked up from a newspaper. It must've been one of the newspapers I saw in the news rack, because it seemed to continue the headline with the words MY RAW WISHES. But I didn't see the rest of it. Maybe it wasn't the same newspaper, and the headline wasn't about somebody's wishes being raw. What could that even mean, wishes being raw? Then I thought maybe the connecting word was SEAMY: hot day in seamy raw wishes, which made even less sense. Then I said to myself, Stop making things make sense, it's only a dream. No, it can't be a dream, otherwise I wouldn't be thinking that maybe it is. But maybe it can be a dream and I'm only dreaming I'm thinking.

The man put the paper down and stared blindly out the window, though not exactly at me. I rapped on the window again, but he didn't seem to see me or hear me. I wondered if the darkness had been reversed. I mean, anyone outside could look in, but nobody inside could see out.

I cupped my hands against the glass and shouted, "Where's the door?"

I guess he didn't hear me. "How do I get in?" I shouted.

He returned to his newspaper, but this time he kept it flat on the table and I didn't see the headline at all. By now I was ravenous with hunger and I thought about finding a brick and smashing the window. With my new-found streetwise courage, I could do it. But I couldn't find a brick. I looked up and down the street, or down and up the street, whichever it is, and no bricks. No rocks, pieces of broken concrete or lumber or anything to break a window with. I realized how clean the street was, how free of debris, except for smashed news racks. No wonder I couldn't find any quarters.

I returned to the restaurant window. The bald man had got up from his table and was heading toward the back. He'd left his newspaper on the table. If I got inside before he returned I could grab the newspaper and finally read the entire headline. I drew my right fist back and dashed it against the window with all my strength.

But the window didn't make a sound. It should've cracked at least. Instead my third and fourth fingers fell off and they weren't even completely necrotic. The necrosis had only reached halfway to the first knuckles. But what good is a right hand with only a thumb and a pinky? I could form the sign of the cuckold, the cornuto, the gypsy's curse. But I could've done that, anyway, when I still had all five fingers. So, as much as I tried to look on the bright side, I knew I had gained nothing losing three. I leaned my head against the window and closed my eyes. I was sure no one inside could see. But I was wrong.

When I opened my eyes, I saw them all staring directly at me. Some of them even pointed. I cupped my hands against the glass and shouted, "Let me in." At that, they all returned to their food, their newspapers, their conversations. I walked farther down, or maybe up, the street looking for another restaurant. It was a long street, so it must've had many restaurants and some of them might be more hospitable then the last one. Maybe, at the last one, they hadn't let me in because all the tables were taken. It couldn't have been how I looked, since no one could see me. Or maybe they could see me only when I pressed my face against the window, with my eyes closed and my cornuto cocked. Maybe that's what I had to do. Stand outside and pretend to cry like a baby so they would notice me.

Except even when they noticed me, they wouldn't let me in. Maybe they couldn't let me in. Maybe they were born inside and would die there and had never left the restaurant and never would, customers, servers, cooks, cashiers, managers, assistant managers and everybody else trapped inside forever. If they had let me in, maybe I never would've got out again. But at least I would've had enough to eat.

Then again maybe not. I realized I didn't have any money to pay the check, not even a single quarter. Suddenly I felt relieved they didn't let me in. I might've been trapped inside and starved to death surrounded by all that food. If all the tables were filled with customers, I would've starved standing up.

I kept walking up, or maybe down, the street. I walked for a long time and then suddenly, on my right, the street opened up into a huge parking area. I knew it was on my right, since the parking area was closer to my two-fingered hand than to my five-fingered one and I knew my two-fingered hand, what was left of it, was my right hand.

Unless I had switched hands. I've heard of that happening, though it had never happened to me, that I know of. Or maybe what people mean when they talk about switching hands, is that they switch not their hands, but the things they hold in their hands. If that's what they mean, why don't they say so? Who do they think they're kidding? The more I thought about that, the angrier I got. I reminded myself to calm down, otherwise I would just keep getting angrier and I needed to keep a cool head if I wanted to find my way home again.

In the distance toward the far edge of the parking area, almost disappearing in haze, was a line of low buildings. I guessed it was a strip mall. A few cars were parked near the buildings, but all the parking spaces everywhere else were empty. Thousands of empty parking spaces were marked in broad, white lines on the asphalt. I started walking toward the strip mall and walked for a long time, but the mall didn't get any closer. I looked up at the sun to estimate the time, but it was hard to locate the sun because the clouds were flitting by too fast and the sun was strobing and I'd get dizzy when I tried to look toward it. But eventually I guessed the time was a little past noon.

That surprised me, because it had been a little past noon when I left home. I thought I had been walking for hours, but the sun was telling me I had been out only a few minutes. If I had been out only a few minutes, there must've been something wrong with my sense of time. Or maybe the sun had stopped moving. But that was silly. The sun couldn't stop moving. Maybe the earth stopped going around its axis. But that was silly, too. If the earth had stopped going around its axis the seas would be flooding the continents and the atmosphere flying off into space. I don't know how I knew that, but I was pretty sure I did.

And maybe that's why the clouds were flitting by so fast. The atmosphere was preparing to launch into space, the oceans to overwhelm the continents. So far I didn't see any giant tidal waves flooding the parking lot. But maybe tidal waves just took longer.

I broke into a dogtrot, trying to reach the strip mall before the world came to an end. I'm not sure why I cared so much. What difference would it have made whether or not I got there before the world ended? Maybe I just wanted to die with a full stomach. But I knew everyone had to have a goal in life, even if it was only to reach the mall in time. Having a goal is what makes life worth living, regardless of the goal. Encouraged by that thought, I broke into a run. And pretty soon the strip mall seemed a little closer. Then suddenly I was there.

I must've run really fast those last few miles, because it hardly seemed to take any time at all to cross them. But maybe I was right the first time, my sense of time was all screwed up. In any case, doesn't that prove how good it is to have a goal, no matter what?

You could see through the windows of the shops in the mall, and you could walk through the doors. In fact, some shops had doors hanging off the hinges. The entire strip mall looked abandoned. I finally came to a restaurant, but there was no furniture in the dining area, no grills in the kitchen, only dusty counters. I inspected the cars parked outside. Some of them might have been there a long time, but a few could've arrived recently. One of them was still ticking from the heat of its engine. I looked around for people but didn't see any. I even called out a couple of times, but the only response I heard was the rushing of the wind.

I finally came to a fountain in a courtyard surrounded by empty shops. The fountain was dry and its basin was littered with trash. I sat down on the edge of the basin and tried to think through my predicament. But my thinking recently had not amounted to much, had only given me a headache, or maybe several headaches all at once, and I was losing confidence in thinking. Maybe it had never amounted to much. Maybe my thinking was the cause of all my troubles. Not that there's anything wrong with thinking. It just has to be the right kind of thinking. That was the hard part. Getting the thought just right so you don't have to be ashamed, frustrated or regretful afterwards, with a head full of headaches.

I plucked out a leaflet from a pile of trash in the basin of the fountain. It had just two words printed on it in large block letters that filled the whole page: EAT ME. Obviously some kind of cynical joke at my expense. I started getting angry again and threw down the leaflet. Then I thought, It's stupid getting angry, it's not something worth getting angry about. And then it suddenly occurred to me that I should take the leaflet literally.

I don't know where that thought came from. Just another idea out of nowhere, I guess. I was getting suspicious of my ideas out of nowhere, but I picked up the leaflet, anyway, and tore it into small bits and began eating the bits one at a time. I couldn't taste anything, not even the dry, rough taste of paper. My mouth didn't even have the sensation of being filled with anything, but after I had finished eating the bits of torn leaflet, I no longer felt hunger. In fact, I felt satisfyingly full. For the first time that afternoon (if afternoon it was) I almost felt as if someone were watching out for me. So I sat there awhile feeling grateful to whoever had sent me that leaflet. I closed my eyes and gratefully listened to the rising and falling rush of wind.

When I opened them I saw a little girl standing in front of me licking an ice cream cone. My belly was so full, the sight of that ice cream cone made me nauseous. I looked around the courtyard and back at the little girl. She wore baggy jeans turned up at the cuffs and a yellow tee shirt with some kind of cute animal drawn on the chest. The cute animal looked somewhat like my right forefinger just after it had fallen off, except the cute animal was dark red. A stubby, red salamander or giant bedbug glutted with blood.

"Where's your mother?" I said.

With a little pink tongue she gave a few more silent licks to her cone, and then she said, "Are you a pervert?"

She laughed and ran away. I was so astonished at the question, I just sat there for a long time. What kind of parent would teach a little kid to say that to a complete stranger? Then I grew afraid the child's mother would report me and send the cops after me. I don't know why I thought that. I guess the day was making me paranoid. I got up and hurried out of the courtyard, in the opposite direction the child had taken. But I never ran into her, or her mother, or anybody. Maybe I had just imagined her. But that seemed unlikely. I still remembered her vividly, and the sound of her voice. Imagination can't be that vivid, nor the feeling of shame and fear when she asked me if I was a pervert. Or at least *my* imagination can't be that vivid. Or maybe it can. I began thinking, Put her in a dark green uniform with the name (whatever it was) of the delivery service stitched across a shirt pocket, she'd look like the little man who delivered that hatbox (if that's what it was). Maybe that was my problem, not thinking too much, but imagining too vividly. Suddenly the fullness in my stomach made me want to throw up.

Maybe the leaflet had actually poisoned me. What a fool I was to think someone had been watching out for me. Nobody was watching out for me, nobody cared about me, there wasn't anything out there except a world full of ill will and indifference. I started cussing whoever had sent the leaflet, and then I did throw up. In a dried-out flower bed.

Maybe something fine would grow out of that puddle of vomit and soggy leaflet bits seeping in the dry dirt, because it looked like nothing else ever had. So why not look on the bright side? After that I began to feel better. I wasn't even very hungry. Not after that.

I felt water drops on my forehead and looked up at the sky. The clouds hardly looked like rain clouds. But the drops kept coming down harder and faster. Maybe the wind was bringing water drops from someplace else. Maybe from a nearby fountain with real water. I realized I was thirsty, and eating the leaflet had made me thirstier. I faced into the wind to look for the source of the water drops, but the wind kept gusting every which way, so I couldn't tell where the water was coming from. The drops were coming down so thick, I was soon soaked through, and I stood under a store awning to wait for the rain to let up, if rain it was. And it definitely looked like rain, even though the clouds didn't seem like rain clouds, scudding by so fast. Maybe this was a forerunner of the tidal wave that would soon flood the earth. In that case, the water drops should've tasted salty like the sea, but these drops were sweet.

I lifted my mouth to the sky to quench my thirst, and suddenly the rain stopped. All I got were a few drops dripping from the awning. The top of the awning must've been dirty, because these last drops tasted foul and gritty, like mud and rust and something bitter. I continued walking through the mall. Streams of dirty water flowed across the courtyards, and foul water over-brimmed the basins of fountains and dripped off awnings and buildings.

The mall was a labyrinth of courtyards and porticos and abandoned shops that seemed to go on forever, and I could hardly tell them all apart. Maybe I was just walking in circles, and the mall was much smaller than I had thought. But in that case, I should've come back to the parking lot by now. Once I got to the parking lot, I could easily make my way back to the street and continue on up it, or down it, till I got home.

Well, maybe not so easily. I remembered how far the mall was from the street. I guessed the street would be equally far from the mall. But maybe I was being too logical there. Just because the mall was a certain distance from the street, that didn't mean the street had to be the same distance from the mall, did it? After all, the last time I crossed it, a big part of that distance was just a matter of attitude. If I had the right attitude I could probably make short shrift of that parking lot. I don't know why I said "short shrift". I don't even know what that means. Is there such a thing as a long shrift? How about a medium-sized shrift? Or maybe shrifts come in one-size-fits-all. But, whatever, a hopeful, optimistic, positive attitude should get me home before I knew it, whatever the size of the shrift. I only had to find the parking lot. Maybe the right attitude would get me there.

But getting the right attitude was as hard as finding something to drink. Even harder, because I was surrounded by dirty water, and I could've drunk it if I didn't mind drinking dirty water. Then I heard something in the distance, over the sound of the wind. It could've been music, someone playing a radio, many people talking all at once, or all these things at the same time. I tried to follow the sound, but the wind kept whipping it back and forth, and I couldn't tell which way the sound was coming from. If I went in any one direction for very long, it would grow fainter, no matter which way I went. Or maybe I only thought I was going in one direction, when actually I was just going in circles. If I had a piece of chalk, I could mark my progress through the mall and at least find out if I was repeating my steps.

But then it might rain again, and the rain would wash off the chalk marks. Or maybe that was just my bad attitude. I needed to keep looking on the bright side of things. Besides, these speculations were pointless, since it was probably just as hard to find a piece of chalk as it was to find a drink of clean water. Suddenly the sound grew louder. It was definitely the sound of music and many voices mingled together, and for once the wind held steady long enough for me to follow the sound.

I came upon a large courtyard, larger than the others I had seen so far. A low stage ran along one side of it. On the stage three women were playing saxophones. Three small children of no discernible sex playing banjos. None of them was the kid who asked if I was a pervert. Two violinists, one bass fiddle player, a jazz drummer, a kettle drummer, a conga drummer. A hammered dulcimer player. An impossibly tall, thin man playing a blue guitar. All stood, sat, or pranced on the platform, playing at the same time. Each one playing a different tune, as far as I could tell. Or maybe it was the same tune, but I was too distracted by my own thoughts to be able to hear it properly. Maybe it was some kind of straight-ahead post-modern, or maybe even post-post-modern, arrangement of something. Whatever that means. Another idea out of nowhere, I guess.

But for a moment I thought I could hear, borne on the wind, a phrase from *Moonlight Sonata* coming from the hammered dulcimer. A moment later one of the saxophone players picked up the phrase. Not that I know anything about music. In fact, I don't know why I thought I recognized the tune. I heard snatches of other familiar tunes from the kids playing banjos. But I have a poor head for song titles, and I wasn't sure of their names. The bass player wasn't even playing. Eyes closed, propped against his instrument, he seemed half asleep. I wondered how anyone could sleep through all that. I couldn't make out what the violinists or the man with the blue guitar was playing. Or if they were playing anything at all, even while their bows and fingers flew rapidly over the strings of their instruments. As for the drummers, each one seemed to be drumming to a different marcher.

In the middle of the courtyard, several couples were slow-dancing at different tempos. A large crowd around them swayed to the music, somebody's music, anyway, but not any music I heard from the stage. Maybe the crowd wasn't swaying to any music at all. I approached them, but a large man intercepted me and said something. I couldn't hear him over the noise and said something back. He said something louder.

Finally I shouted, "How do you know you're not dreaming?"

He screamed, "Because I can't get to sleep."

I started toward the crowd again, but the big man grabbed my arm and spun me around. This time I understood him.

"It's a private party," he screamed.

I was about to ask him where I could get a bite to eat, when a young woman came up to us. Just then the band stopped playing. I wondered how they could each play different tunes in different tempos and know when to stop at exactly the same time. The sudden silence was eerie. All I could hear was the wind and the shuffling of the dancing couples, who kept on dancing even after the music had stopped.

The young woman said, "He's with me," and hooked her arm through mine and pulled me toward the dancing couples. She said, "You owe me a dance."

"I can't dance," I said.

"Oh, just let your feet listen to the beat."

I never thought my feet could hear that well, but I was willing to let them try. She put my right hand on her waist. She didn't seem bothered that my hand only had two fingers, and most of the hand had turned purple and had swollen nearly twice its normal size. She took my left hand in her right hand. Her hand was tiny, dry and wrinkled. But it felt like a real hand, and I couldn't have been dreaming it.

"I don't hear the beat," I said. In fact, I only heard the wind and the shuffling of many feet. My feet didn't hear the beat either, because they weren't moving at all. I wondered if I would hear it when the band started playing again. She swayed gently back and forth in front of me.

"You're really good," she said. "You're an amazing dancer." She had a long, thin face and great, unblinking eyes and straight brown hair draped like a silken shawl over her shoulders.

"You look dry," I said. "Did you stay out of the rain?"

"Oh, nothing ever rains on my party," she said.

"I got soaked," I said. "Just over there." But I didn't feel damp any more. It must've been a long time ago when I had got soaked, and I must've lost track of time. I started nodding in the direction I thought I had come from, to show her where I got rained on. But as I looked around, every direction seemed the same. I wasn't even sure the stage was in the same place as when I entered the courtyard. I said, "Where can I get a bite to eat around here?"

"Are you hungry?"

I wondered why she would ask if I was hungry, after I had just asked where I could get a bite to eat. Maybe she thought my question was just academic curiosity, but I don't remember ever having been academically curious about anything, or at least not about getting a bite to eat. Or non-academically curious for that matter. But maybe I was once. Or maybe not, who knows?

Or maybe around here nobody ever ate, but I hoped they liked to know where they could if they wanted to. I was about to say yes, I was hungry, when suddenly another spasm of nausea passed through me. After vomiting up the leaflet, I had lost my appetite and then thought I was regaining it, but now I was no longer so sure.

She said, "I'm on a diet, I've never eaten out around here."

"You're thin as a rail," I said. I meant to compliment her, but she suddenly looked troubled. She never took her large, dark eyes off mine, but her eyebrows drew close together. To change the subject, I said, "So how do *you* know you're not dreaming?"

She said something, but just then the band started up, and I couldn't hear her answer, which must've pleased her, because she stopped frowning and smiled up at me. To please her, I smiled back, which seemed to please her even more, though I felt frustrated I never heard her answer.

We danced awhile without speaking, or rather she swayed gently in front of me, while I stood without moving my feet. Her gentle swaying seemed the only thing around that had a definite tempo. But soon the music fell in with the same tempo as her movements. Even the bass fiddle player had awoken and was plucking his strings at the same tempo. I looked around, and the other dancers and spectators had also fallen in with the music. It was as if her movements had orchestrated everybody else's movements — dancers', spectators', musicians'. I guess their feet finally started listening to the beat, and the musicians must've been listening to it, too, but my feet were as deaf as ever. Maybe my feet were just tired from all their walking, after I had left home this afternoon.

But then I wondered if it had been this afternoon when I had left home. Maybe it had been some other afternoon. I bent down close to her ear and said, "What day is it today?"

She raised her mouth close to my ear, and I felt the delicate, moist whispers of her breath in my ear, but I couldn't make out what she was saying, except the word "moon". Maybe she was talking about *Moonlight Sonata*, which I thought I had heard when I entered the courtyard. The feel of her breath in my ear suddenly aroused me, and I had a huge hard-on. I pulled her close and held her tight. Her body moved back and forth against mine, and I ejaculated. If I had been dreaming, that should've awakened me. I've never been able to sleep through something like that. Maybe that's how I knew I wasn't dreaming. Then again, in a dream, there's a first time for everything, isn't there? Then again, maybe not.

She seemed not to notice what I had done, or what had happened to me — is there really any difference? — and just looked up at me from her great, unblinking eyes. When I released her she stepped back, still swaying. It occurred to me that the music would never stop till she stopped swaying. An eternity of that could get tiresome, and I wondered if I should make my escape now. But my feet wouldn't move, and I couldn't have made my escape even if I had wanted to. Maybe I didn't want to, and that's why my feet didn't move. Or maybe moving my feet is not something I can do, but something that has to happen to me. I mean, if there's really any difference.

Just then the music stopped, and silence came over us again. This time the couples stopped shuffling, and even the wind stopped blowing. My partner stood still in front of me. She seemed to be waiting for me to do something or to say something.

"Do you come here often?" I said.

"Do you?" she said.

"I just did."

"You just came here often?"

"Where do you live?" I said, confused by her question.

"Over there." I thought she nodded in the direction she mentioned, but I wasn't sure which way that was.

"I feel like we've known each other — I mean the way you came up and said, He's with me."

Frowning she said, "You *are* with me."

I didn't know why she was frowning. I wondered if I had offended her.

I said, "Well, you have the advantage over me. I feel like I should know you, but..."

She said, "You don't know me, you don't know me at all."

"But *you* know me?"

She seemed puzzled and didn't say anything. Maybe she was puzzled because she didn't know the answer. But then she gave a tiny shake of her head, not as if to say she didn't know me, but as if to say the answer was too obvious to mention. Maybe she was puzzled because she didn't understand why I didn't know the answer. Well, if it was so simple, why didn't she just tell me? I was about to tell her that, when I felt water drops on my head.

I said, "It's raining again."

She shook her head. "It never rains here."

"What do you think this is?"

We both started to get wet. Her hair gleamed with drops of water, thousands of tiny pearls glinting on silk. I grabbed her arm and pulled her over to the side of the courtyard where we stood in the entrance of one of the abandoned shops. The band started playing again, the same discordant noises I first heard when I arrived at the party. I said, "How can they play in this downpour, it'll ruin their instruments."

"It never rains here."

"What do you call this?" The scudding clouds still didn't look like rain clouds, but I had given up the idea that the world was coming to an end right away. In any case, I could accept that she didn't mean the same thing by rain that I meant, but I wasn't going to accept that it wasn't raining. I wondered how I could argue the point if she didn't know what "rain" meant. Or at least didn't know what it meant to me.

We were standing in front of a bicycle shop. It was mostly empty, littered and covered in dust, but a couple of bikes were still stuck in their racks. I dragged her inside. The tires were flat on one of the bikes, but the other one was in pretty good shape, though dusty. It wasn't even chained to the rack, and I wondered why no one had taken it.

I said, "Ever gone biking in the rain?" She shook her head. I pulled the bike out of the rack and said, "Here's your chance to find out what it's like." She tried pulling out the one with the flat tires, but that one for some reason was still chained to the rack.

I said, "We'll take this one. You can ride on the handlebars. Ever ridden on handlebars in the rain before?" She shook her head, and we went outside. It had stopped raining.

She said, "I told you."

I was almost disappointed. Now she wouldn't know what it was like to ride in the rain on handlebars. The band had stopped playing. They must've taken a break because they were no longer on the stage. The banjos and violins and the blue guitar had disappeared, but the larger instruments were still there, dripping wet. Most of the party guests had drifted away. A few couples still swayed together in the middle of the courtyard in the rain-dripping silence.

I straddled the bike and patted the handlebars and said, "Hop on." She shook her head.

"I can't leave the party."

"The party's over." She kept shaking her head, and I said, "Suit yourself."

I set off across the courtyard on the bike. And a moment later, she was sitting on the handlebars. She must've hopped on when I wasn't looking. I'm not sure how that could've happened, since she was sitting right in front of me now, and I don't remember having looked away. The wind was blowing her long hair in my face, and I couldn't see where I was going. I was just guessing I was heading back to the street and hoped I wouldn't bump into anything.

I said, "Help me navigate this thing." But she didn't say anything. She seemed to sit easily on the handlebars, perfectly balanced, as if she'd been doing it all her life. I wondered why she said she had never done it. But maybe she meant she'd never done it in the rain.

She must've weighed next to nothing. I pedaled faster and faster, thinking now I could leave this mall behind in no time flat and get back on the street and get home again. I thought, I'll take her home with me, and I began thinking of all the things we'd do together. You want to party, I'll show you how to party, I thought. But first we'd open the hatbox together. I no longer cared whom it belonged to. With her beside me I'd be able to open it.

And soon the mall came to an end, but not at the street, as I had hoped. It ended abruptly at the foot of a smooth, concrete embankment that rose about twenty, thirty feet in the air and stretched in both directions as far as I could see. I heard the roar and rush of motor traffic on top, but I couldn't see anything up there. She hopped off the handlebars and scrambled up the embankment.

I tried following her, pushing the bike up with me, but it kept sliding back. I didn't want to leave the bike, but I couldn't take it with me, not if I was going to follow her, and I wanted to follow her. After all, she seemed to know where she was going. I called up to her to wait for me, but she had disappeared over the top.

She probably couldn't hear me over the noise of the traffic. Even as I thought that, the noise got much louder. It's almost as if I had made it louder just by thinking how loud it was.

I dropped the bike and tried climbing up the embankment, but I couldn't get a firm grip on the concrete. Maybe it was because my right hand was too swollen and only had two fingers. I tried again and again but kept sliding back, and just then my right hand fell off. On two fingers it scurried up the slope. It looked like a fat little headless man, all bloated and bruised, and quickly disappeared after her.

I had already blubbered too much for the loss of my fingers and had no tears left for the loss of a hand. Besides, I always felt ashamed crying over such a stupid thing, so I sat down dry-eyed at the foot of the embankment next to the bike. Hoping she'd notice I wasn't following. Hoping she'd come back for me. Maybe she'd bring back my hand. I waited a long time, but she never showed.

I hopped on the bike and rode it along the foot of the embankment. The bike was a lot more sluggish now without her sitting on the handlebars. It was as if her body had made the trip across the mall much lighter. But without her sitting on the handlebars, the pedaling got harder and finally it got so hard I had to stop. I got off the bike and let it drop to the pavement, and continued on foot.

From time to time I looked back at the bike to see how far I had gone. But also because I missed riding it. For a while it didn't seem I had gone but a few feet from it. Then the last time I looked back, it had disappeared from view altogether. I wondered how I could have suddenly gone so far in those few moments. But maybe I had just lost track of time as I was walking away from it.

I walked on for a long time and came to an opening in the embankment: a narrow, unlit pedestrian underpass tunneling under the causeway. Deep in the tunnel a tiny, brilliant spot of light. If the light was at the end of the tunnel, the causeway on top must've been much wider than I had thought. Wide enough for a dozen lanes of traffic and many broad meridians, medians and midways between the lanes.

I entered the underpass. I wondered if the light would recede as I approached it. By now I was used to the day's little tricks, so maybe my entering the tunnel was just an act of defiance of them, even while I thought the light was an illusion and the tunnel had no end. I might've said life's little tricks, but I don't know if I had lived it long enough to judge. Or maybe I had lived it long enough, but couldn't remember much about my life before I had left home this afternoon.

The light at the end of the tunnel grew. So far no tricks. The noise overhead fell to a muffled roar. Sometimes a heavy vehicle at high speed passed right over my head, making a sharp explosive sound and knocking particles of dirt off the ceiling of the underpass. The ground began to slope downward slightly.

Rainwater from outside must've drained into the tunnel, and I was soon walking ankle-deep in water. The water got deeper, and soon I was knee-deep. I wondered if I'd have to swim part of the way. That worried me because I wasn't a good swimmer. I don't know how I knew that. Instinct, maybe, like knowing you're not going to fly when you jump off a building. It's not something you need to experience to know you won't be good at it.

It was too dark in the tunnel to see the water, but the water had a foul smell. Maybe it wasn't rainwater at all, but leakage from a broken sewer line. So the day, or whatever it was, still had some tricks. I should've known it would come up with something I never anticipated. So then I started to get mad, and a moment later I was standing at the entrance to the other end of the tunnel, blinking in the bright sunlight.

By now I knew that just getting mad wouldn't solve my problems, but it might make the day, or whatever it was, change the scenery. And on this side of the causeway the sun was very bright. Not a cloud in the sky or breath of wind. No sound of traffic up on the causeway, either. Maybe the traffic only moved along the other side. I was facing open countryside, fields, and low hills in the distance, and a few trees here and there, and a very eerie silence. I might've thought I had gone deaf, if I hadn't heard my own footsteps. Just to be sure, I said aloud, "Hello?" and laughed at the absurdity. My voice sounded strange in the silence, my laughter stranger still, as if they came from someone else, and yet they sounded too close, as if they came from me.

The sun had moved a little past noon, I guessed. I couldn't be sure, since it was too bright to look at and locate its position precisely. My shadow pointed behind me at the mouth of the tunnel, so at least I knew I was facing west. But it wasn't much of a shadow, just two tiny spits of darkness sticking out from my heels. But I didn't know which way was home. I was pretty sure home wasn't in the country. Last time I looked it was downtown.

But downtown was someplace behind me through the tunnel. I turned around and looked through the narrow darkness at the distant, dim, flickering light on the other side, but the thought of walking back through that dark water suddenly filled me with dread. This warm, bright countryside seemed a lot more hospitable. Maybe I could even settle down here if I never found my way home. I don't know why I thought that. It's as if I was suddenly convinced I couldn't go home again.

# ION EYE MASS HARD WITH YAWS

I headed west across the fields toward the hills. Every now and then, I checked my shadow just to make sure I stayed the course. I couldn't tell if the fields were cultivated or not. Sometimes I walked along straight furrows of planted crops, and a moment later I would run into wide patches overgrown with weeds.

I couldn't identify the crops, either. Not that I knew all that much about agriculture. Some of these crop plants looked vaguely like lettuce. I knew something about lettuce, since I had seen plenty in the produce market. I mean, if I had ever been in a produce market. I don't know what made me think I had. Maybe I hadn't.

Anyway, the leaves on some of these lettuce-like plants had folded back, and sometimes I thought I saw in them eyeballs staring up at me. I'm sure I had seen that in a movie once — eyeballs staring at you from inside a head of lettuce, or some such thing. But I couldn't remember which movie it was. The eyeballs always meant someone was watching. Or maybe the lettuce, or whatever it was, was sending signals ahead through its underground root system to warn the local munchkins you were coming.

But it was probably all a trick of sunlight. I didn't really want to stop and find out. I was hungry again and might have eaten some lettuce but I wasn't really sure it was lettuce, and those eyeballs, if they were eyeballs and not tricks of the light, had definitely put me off my feed, despite my hunger.

Soon I ran into a thicket of brambles and thistles and had to detour. I guess I turned north-east now, but the ground was uneven here, and I couldn't quite make out which way my shadow pointed. Then I ran into another impenetrable thicket. No matter which way I turned I kept running into thickets. Even if I had wanted to, I couldn't have found my way back to the underpass now. I took back all the nice things I said about the day on this side of the causeway. The day on this side was as treacherous as it had been on the other side, maybe worse. And it was still only a little past noon.

I don't know how I had wandered into the trap, hemmed in by brambles and thistles on every side. Maybe I was so focused on what was ahead of me, I didn't notice what was going on behind me. It was as if the thicket had silently closed in behind me. It rose above my head and, if I had tried to climb over it, it would've collapsed under my weight and I'd be trapped in the tangle, pierced to the bone with thistles. I guess they finally got what they wanted, now that I was their prisoner (whoever they were). I'd just have to sit and wait for whatever came next. Maybe I could get mad again, and that would change the scenery. But I couldn't count on getting mad. Getting mad would only solve the problem by creating a bigger problem.

I sat down on the ground, the hot sun beating down on me, and I grew thirsty again. I guess my chances of finding water out here were even less than back at the mall. It didn't look as if the plants had been given much water, either. I hadn't noticed before but the plants looked as dry as tinder, yellow and brittle. Something gleamed in the dirt nearby. At first I thought it was another eyeball, but without the lettuce. Maybe a head of lettuce that had dried up and turned to dust, leaving its eyeball behind.

I picked it up and rubbed the dirt off. It was a bit of broken glass, convex on one side, nearly flat on the other. Spots of brilliant light danced around the clearing when I hefted the piece of glass in my hand.

With the glass I focused a spot of sunlight on my right arm, where necrosis had advanced above the wrist. I didn't feel any pain when the hairs on my arm smoked and frizzled in the heat of the spot of sunlight. I wondered if I could stop the advance of necrosis by burning off the rest of my arm. But I wasn't ready to try such remedies yet.

I focused the spot of sunlight on a nearby shrub, which smoked, frizzled and soon burst into flames. Maybe I could burn my way out of my prison, if I didn't burn myself up first. That would solve the problem of necrosis, if I burned myself up, but I wasn't ready for that remedy, either, so I hoped I didn't.

Soon I was surrounded by a wall of flames. For some reason I didn't feel any hotter than I had been when I was sitting quietly in the sun, feeling thirsty. Smoke rose straight up, so I was breathing clean air and, in fact, the air didn't even smell smoky. Glowing embers floated down around me. So much fire should roar, but this one didn't make a sound and silently moved away from me on all sides, leaving behind smoking, black ground. I put the piece of glass in my pocket and waited. I thought I'd have to wait a long time for the ground to cool. But before I knew it, I had crossed the burned-out field, and came to a stand of shady trees.

They looked like oak trees. Not that I knew much about trees, but these had dome-shaped crowns and spreading branches, and the ground was littered with acorns. At least I thought they were acorns. They looked like the heads of cut-off penises, but they were woody-hard and greenish-brown. I must've read someplace that acorns were edible, and I was still hungry, but I lost my appetite looking at them. This wasn't the first time today I had lost my appetite. Maybe I could quench my appetite just by looking at things that made me lose it. I was sure the day still held many nauseating things.

I sat down in the cool shade of the tree, brushing aside the acorns, and looked across the burned-out field at the clearing that had held me prisoner. It was a small, brown patch surrounded by acres of blackness. The blackness had stopped smoking, which surprised me, since I thought it would take days to cool it off. Maybe it really had taken days. Maybe the sun had set and risen two or three times already, and I hadn't even noticed. But it was still a little past noon. I mean, judging from the shadows of the trees. I'm sure I would've noticed something about the passing of days, however screwed up my sense of time was: a momentary glint of sunset, a glimmer of moonlight, moments of darkness during that passage of two or three nights. No, this had to be the same day I left home.

In the distance, barely visible, a thin, dark line cut across the horizon. It looked like the edge of the world. Not that I knew what the edge of the world looked like, or even if there was such a thing, but that's how I imagined it would be if the world had an edge. It took me a moment to realize it was only the causeway.

I must've come a long way since I came out of the tunnel, ten or twelve miles at least. I tried to remember how long it normally took me to walk ten or twelve miles. Not that I normally walked that far. I fact I don't remember walking at all before I left home this afternoon. But I guess if I had walked ten or twelve miles it could've taken four or five hours, not allowing for the time I was trapped inside the bramble patch.

The shadows should've been much longer now, but the sun was still high overhead. This had to be the same day, a little past noon. I still had plenty of time left in the day to get home. Maybe the day was doing me a favor, holding up the passage of time, delaying the onset of darkness while I found my way. Besides, I always liked to explore things, and this countryside held plenty of things to explore. Actually, I don't know if I always liked to explore things. Maybe I'm just saying that, and only think I liked to explore things because I think I'm supposed to like it, or maybe because I have to like it if I want to get home.

I turned my back on the distant causeway and started through the trees. The trees gave way to a rugged, gravelly slope, huge boulders all around. I paused and turned and looked down toward the grove of trees, but they were hidden behind a brow of the hill. I couldn't see the causeway or the burned-out patch, either. In fact, from a distance all the fields looked green or freshly plowed, not the dry tinder I had crossed long ago, or not so long ago.

I must've got turned around climbing up the hill. Maybe I was climbing up the other side of the hill, but then I got confused and thought I was still climbing up this side. Whatever *this side* means. Maybe when I got to the top I'd see all the familiar landmarks on the other side. Then I'd go back down the other side to the grove of trees and head off in a more comfortable direction. Except I didn't really know which way was more comfortable. But at least now I knew I had all day to find out, since the day was so generous with its time.

I struggled on up the hill. I couldn't see the top from here. Maybe there was no top, and the hill just kept on going up forever. But I guess even hills must have a top. Or maybe not, what do I know. I turned and looked back. I think I heard somewhere that when you look back it's not your past you see, it's your future. I wonder if that means your past lies ahead. Maybe that's why I can't remember mine.

Whatever. I seemed to have come up a long way, longer than I had thought. A vast landscape stretched hundreds of miles into a yellow haze. Even the ground at the foot of the mountain had grown indistinct, details of trees and fields softly focused through a haze. Not a very promising future, if that's what it was. I wondered if I'd be stuck on this mountainside forever, the top always too far above me, the ground receding ever faster from me.

But then for a moment I felt as big as the mountain — or at least *a* mountain, since I didn't really know how big this mountain was — and I thought I was looking down at a miniature landscape below me. Then I looked at my feet, which were huge, only inches below my chin, and my body between ankle and neck had vanished, and I was nothing but a head with feet.

Of course my feet could carry me to the top, but without legs they didn't carry me quickly, and I must've spent days toiling up the slope, though the sun still stood at a little past noon. Then I rounded a boulder looming over me and I realized I was there, I had reached the top, and my legs had suddenly grown back. I don't know why they (whoever they were) had to play that stupid trick on me, taking my legs away from me like that. I guess they wanted me to give up and stay there forever on the mountainside. Well, too bad for them because here I was, on top of the world.

But the other side was not the familiar landscape I had walked across. A long, grassy slope descended gently to a valley of lakes and woods. A gleaming river coiled through the valley. I walked down through wet grass, and soon my pants were soaked to the knees. It must've rained here recently, maybe the same rain that had drenched me at the strip mall, but I didn't see a cloud in the sky, and I wondered how the grass could've stayed so wet in the warm sunshine of this eternal afternoon.

Maybe it wasn't eternal. All things end, for time must have a stop. I wondered where I got that idea. Maybe I confused it with: the mountain must have a top. I repeated it aloud, "time must have a stop," just to make sure how it sounded. My voice sounded strange to me, as if it came from someone else, and the thought still didn't sound like something I would think of. For time must have a stop — that didn't even make any sense. Time stops or has *to* stop or comes to a stop but it can't *have* a stop. But somehow I had thought it. I didn't think it was something someone else was thinking. There was no one else around but me to do the thinking here. Maybe it was just one of those ideas that came to me, the way the idea came to me when I left home and started asking people, How do you know you're not dreaming.

Maybe that's what got me lost this afternoon. Maybe if I had kept my mouth shut I'd be home by now. But I just didn't see the connection between asking a simple question and ending up on this hillside. Or time stopping and having a stop.

The wet grass reminded me of my thirst. I kneeled on the ground and tried to shake water into my mouth. Somehow the drops missed my mouth but landed everywhere else on my face. I put a clump of grass in my mouth and sucked on it, but it must've been a dry clump. I grabbed another clump glittering with dew, but I must've shaken off all the drops before I got the clump in my mouth. All around me grass dripped with water, but one way or another I couldn't get any water in my mouth. I finally gave up and got to my feet.

I walked on down for a while and came to a lookout, where I saw part of the valley I hadn't seen from the top. A weathered sign lay in the wet grass. The sign said

LOOKOUT

I bent down and looked at it more closely. It actually said

LOOK OUT

The two words were separated. Or maybe not all that separated. The letters were crudely spaced, so I wasn't sure what was separated from what. Maybe the words were supposed to mean both things, lookout and look out. In any case, the sign had been lying there a long time, nailed to a square post whose base had rotted away. I lifted up one edge and promptly dropped it when I saw worms and beetles swarming over the glistening, black ground beneath. Not that worms and beetles can hurt you. Or maybe they can. I don't know much about worms and beetles. Maybe you can even eat them. I was suddenly hungry again and lifted up the edge a second time, but by this time the worms and beetles had all slithered into the ground.

I straightened up and looked down into the valley, the part I hadn't seen from the mountaintop. I thought I saw a cluster of buildings behind some trees, but I couldn't be sure. Through the boughs of those trees I saw sharp angles and straight vertical lines, patterns that don't exist in nature. Not that I know much about nature. Maybe they do exist in nature. I don't know what made me think they don't.

I continued on down for a long time. It must've taken me all afternoon to reach the bottom. Except it couldn't have, the sun still stood at a little past noon. At the foot of the mountain I came to a narrow stream, a pretty rivulet lined with willows, ferns and moss. I knelt down to drink and cupped some water in my hand, but a foul, bitter stench struck my nose when I brought the hand to my face, a stench like the water in the underpass, only worse.

At first I thought my cupping hand was also starting to rot away, and that's where the stench came from, but then I bent down and sniffed the water in the stream and nearly fainted from the foulness. I wondered how the willows, ferns and moss could survive it. Maybe they weren't real willows, ferns and moss. But they looked real. Not that I know anything about willows, ferns and moss.

I tore off a fern frond and brought it to my nose, but I couldn't smell anything. The only thing I could smell was the water. The stream must've been from a chemical discharge someplace. I got to my feet and walked along the stream. I would've parted ways with the stream, but I guessed it led down to the river, and that cluster of buildings I had seen from the lookout was near the river. And maybe the river water upstream was drinkable. But I didn't know whether the buildings, if they really existed, were upstream or downstream. But at least I had all afternoon to find out, as long as the sun kept standing at a little past noon.

I climbed up on a bluff near the stream, where I had a good view of much of the valley. But I didn't see the river anywhere. That surprised me since, from the mountaintop, it had seemed like a substantial river, visible from just about anywhere in the valley. Maybe this bluff was one of the few places it was not visible from.

I followed the stream down through a shallow gorge where I had to walk in the water. If I could walk in the water of the underpass I could walk in this water, despite the noxious smell. At least this water I could see. The rocks were slippery and loose and I had to step carefully, but soon the gorge opened up into wide, marshy ground, and the stream disappeared into the marsh.

I started walking across the marsh but instantly sank up to my knees in mud and had to slog back to high ground. I skirted along the edge of the marsh, which was bounded by a muddy embankment. There was hardly any solid ground to walk on, and I kept slipping into the bog. But soon the marsh seemed to turn into solid ground. It was covered with tall, coarse grass, and when I stepped on the grass the ground was springy but firm. My one hand brushed against the grass, and I felt a stinging sensation. A moment later a crisscross pattern of welts rose up on the back of my hand and forearm. That surprised me, since so far today I hadn't experienced anything except hunger and thirst and that horrible stench.

I stayed away from the stinging grass and walked along the foot of the muddy embankment. Pretty soon the muddy embankment flattened out to level ground, and fields of stinging grass stretched ahead of me as far as I could see. My shadow pointed straight ahead of me, so I must've been walking east, in the direction I had come from when I came over the mountain. Maybe my climb over that mountain had been completely unnecessary. If I had been paying attention, maybe I could've avoided the climb and gone around the mountain. And ended up on the other side of these fields of stinging grass. Not that I would've wanted to end up there if I had known there was nothing but that grass.

I wondered if I should walk back along the foot of the muddy embankment, cross the stinking stream, and continue on in that direction. But the last time I had tried retracing my steps, I got lost and ended up in the mall. And it was a long way back to the stinking stream, along a treacherous path. One misstep, and I'd slide into the stinging grass, or maybe the bog would swallow me whole.

Stinging grass to my left, stinging grass straight ahead, but to my right was a thickly wooded area. By my calculations, the mountain I had climbed over should be beyond those woods, but I only saw trees there and the cloudless sky beyond them. In fact, I saw no sign of hills or mountains anywhere, no matter which way I looked.

I headed toward the woods, glad to get away from the stinging grass. But at the edge of the woods I paused. There was something peculiar about those woods. Not that I knew anything about woods, but these had a distinctly phony appearance, as if they were some kind of stage scenery: thick, gnarly trees improbably painted in blocks of basic colors, and impenetrable darkness beyond, as if the darkness had been painted on, too. I don't know why it looked like painted scenery. Maybe I had seen a play once.

A faint stench came out of the darkness, like the stench rising from the stinking stream. On a bright day like this, sunlight should've filtered down through the leaves and speckled the forest floor. But this was like looking deep into a cave painted black on plywood.

At first I was amused at all this pretentious stagecraft. "Who do you think you're kidding?" I said aloud to the day. The sound of my voice sounded strange. As if it were someone else's voice coming out of the woods.

And then I thought I'd just grope my way through the woods till I got to the other side, wherever that was, if it was anywhere. But just the thought suddenly terrified me. And then another thought: the power of our love can silence our worst terrors. That thought came to me, and vanished as quickly as it came. It must've been one of those thoughts that couldn't have been mine, so I had no right to keep it, and it somehow knew that. Besides, there was no one else around here to love, except myself. And if that's what I loved, the love wasn't silencing my fear of those dark woods. I'd walk forever through the stinging grass before I'd spend one minute in those woods.

I went back to the edge of the field and tested the ground with my foot. The ground was springy but firm. But not firm enough. Ten feet out, and the crust of springy earth suddenly broke beneath my foot, and I plunged to my knee in fetid mud. I turned back. All the way back to solid ground, the earth kept breaking beneath me. It took a lot longer getting back than going out. Both arms were covered with welts by the time I got there. My right arm, where the rot was advancing beyond the wrist, hardly felt anything, but my left arm was exploding with pain. It felt strange, feeling pain again, after having felt so little. I lay down on the ground and waited for the pain to recede: above me, a brilliant, cloudless sky, the sun a little past noon.

The pain subsided to a dull throb, and then I got up and explored my little island of safe ground: stinging grass on two sides, dark woods on another, on yet another the muddy embankment. I saw no way off the island except the way I had come. Maybe I could walk back to the stinking stream along the top of the muddy embankment. But the dark woods came close to the top edge and I wasn't sure I could walk along the edge without stepping into the darkness of those woods. So I started back along the foot of the embankment.

I saw my shoeprints in the mud going in the opposite direction. So I was sure I couldn't get lost here retracing my steps, I was sure my misgivings were groundless. Certainly not more groundless than the slippery ground I walked on now. I walked, or rather slipped and slid, for a long time. Much longer than I thought I had walked going the other way. Maybe the pain in my arm was slowing me down.

I started to get mad again, mainly mad at myself for being afraid to go through the woods. In this bright sunlight, on this treacherous path, those fears seemed pointless now. I no longer knew what had come over me when I stood at the edge of those woods. It was as if every nightmare I had ever slept through had suddenly overwhelmed my good judgment.

Not that I had shown all that much good judgment today. But at least I'd had enough not to be afraid of anything till I got to the woods. Except maybe the brief dread I had felt after coming through the underpass.

I don't know why I should've been scared then, after the fact. It was just the thought of going back in the tunnel that had scared me, even though I had come out of it without mishap. Other than that, at worst I was mad, frustrated or depressed, but never frightened until I came to the dark woods. And most of the day I hadn't felt much of anything.

Maybe I should've been grateful to those dark woods, forcing me to experience the full range of my emotions. Maybe it was all just good therapy. Whatever that means. I'm sure I've heard about good therapy before, otherwise I wouldn't have mentioned it now, even though I'm not sure what it is. But in any case, it's much better feeling nothing at all. Feeling nothing made it a lot easier walking along that slippery path. So maybe good therapy is overrated.

I went on for a long time, still following my shoeprints, but I never came to the stinking stream. Instead, I came to a narrow boardwalk that crossed the marsh going north, at least according to my shadow. I wondered how I could've missed seeing that boardwalk before. Maybe I was so focused on not sliding off the path that I passed by the boardwalk without noticing it. Then I noticed my shoeprints were pointing the wrong way, coming off the edge of the boardwalk, pointing towards me.

I was sure I had never walked across that boardwalk. If I had walked across it, my shoeprints should've been pointing toward the boardwalk, not away from it. Maybe those shoeprints were not really mine. I bent down and looked at them more closely, and matched them with a fresh pair of shoeprints, and the old ones looked exactly like the fresh ones. Same dimensions, imprint of pattern, depth. Maybe I forgot I had crossed over and came back. But then the shoeprints should've pointed in both directions. Maybe someone was playing tricks on me and having a good laugh at my expense. I considered every scenario I could think of, and none gave me any comfort. The worst thought was, my shoeprints coming back at me implied I hadn't found a way out at the other end of the boardwalk, if the boardwalk had an end.

So I should just sit down here in the mud and do nothing until whatever. I must've been delusional to think I had any control over my life. Maybe I should throw myself into the marsh and see where that took me. Or go back and throw myself on the mercy of the dark woods. Or flay myself to death in the field of stinging grass. But not if it was just another mean-spirited trick. It couldn't hurt to find out, anyway. Although that thought depressed me.

"Why do you keep trying?" I said aloud. My voice sounded strange to my ears, as if it came from someone else. But I kept on talking: "I try not to try, but trying not to try is just another form of trying, and a lot more exhausting." So I guess I answered my own question. Actually it wasn't really a question, since I couldn't have cared less what the answer was. I guess I was just acting out, keeping myself company with the sound of my own voice.

I got up and started across. The boardwalk bucked and wallowed underfoot, though I tried to walk softly. It should've made noises when it did that, maybe smacking the wet mud beneath it, or making loud creaking and thumping sounds. But I heard nothing in the eerie silence. At times it seemed as if it wanted to throw me into the bog. There were no handrails or guide ropes to hang on to, so I got down and crawled on one hand and knees. The boardwalk stopped bucking and wallowing, but started up again when I got to my feet. I guess it wanted me to crawl across, and liked seeing a man all covered in mud and nettle welts, humiliating himself on one hand and knees. But that's silly. It was just a thing made of wood, it couldn't have wanted anything.

Then I wondered how it could see me crawling or trying to walk, what sort of senses it had that could detect how a man moved. Maybe by the way my weight was distributed on its surface. It was probably just some kind of machine. If I looked underneath, I'd find all the gears, cranks, flywheels and motors that made it buck and wallow. Maybe the machine was like some fidgety, mechanical beast that grew quiet when you found the right spot to scratch. Or a horse that could tolerate only a certain kind of rider and would throw anybody else. In that case I should be patient and tolerant and respectful, grateful it was willing to bear me across. Not that I knew anything about animals.

Thinking about animals reminded me how hungry I was. If I saw one I'd strangle it and eat it raw. Or maybe I could start another fire with the piece of glass in my pocket and cook the animal. That thought began to cheer me up. Maybe I could burn up some stinging grass just for the pleasure of watching the evil stuff burn. Except it looked too green to burn. Or burn up the boardwalk, the stupid thing deserved no less. I mean, after I was done crawling over it.

But I hadn't seen any animals at all around here, except worms and beetles up on the mountainside. I hadn't even seen any birds. I wondered where all the birds had flown. This marshland should've been home to all kinds of birds. Maybe the water had been poisoned, and only dark woods and stinging grass could live here. The stinking stream water certainly wasn't drinkable, and it was feeding the marsh. That's probably what was poisoning the marsh and every living thing that was feeding on it. But someone must live around here, because someone had built the boardwalk. Unless the boardwalk had built itself. I wouldn't put it past it, the stupid thing. Or maybe it had been here forever.

I wondered when the ordeal would end, all this crawling on one hand and knees. Maybe never. But probably not never. Whoever was running the show liked to vary the torment. They'd probably get bored just watching me do the same thing over and over again.

I didn't see anything ahead except endless marsh, and here and there clumps of stinging grass. The hills and woods I had seen from the lookout were nowhere in sight. And I'm sure the woods I had seen from the lookout were real woods and not just stage scenery in a play of horror. Sure of it, since I had seen sunlight shining through their boughs and some kind of structure behind them. Or maybe they weren't real woods, or real trees, or real structures, or real light shining down on this place. But that's silly. Even if this was all smoke and mirrors, at least it was real smoke and mirrors. Somewhere behind all the unreality is the reality of the unreality. No matter where you go, no matter how unreal it gets, you can't get away from the reality.

And then suddenly the boardwalk ended. Right in the middle of all the smoke and mirrors, or whatever this was. So that's why my future self had to turn back. If I really had a future self. That thought cheered me up a little — it meant I actually did have a future. But what if I didn't, and my future was probably just another trick of the day, like the shoeprints that pointed only one way.

The mud and clumps of grass ended here where the boardwalk also ended, and blank, brown water stretched ahead of me. I thought I saw far off a flat, muddy shore fading into a hazy horizon. I wondered what happened to the pretty valley I had seen from the mountaintop. But I shouldn't be surprised anymore by anything in this place of smoke and mirrors (if that's what it was), I shouldn't be surprised at all, not on a day like this.

The end of the boardwalk dipped into the brown water. I was still on one hand and knees and peered down over the edge. The end of the boardwalk rested on the shallow lake bottom, which was level as far as I could see, as if it had been paved over with concrete, like the floor of a swimming pool. I lay down flat on my belly and sniffed the water, but it didn't stink, it didn't smell at all. Even normal water has a slight odor of something, but this had nothing.

I was still thirsty, but I didn't drink. This water had brown, scummy things floating in it and brown scum coating the bottom. It felt good to be stretched out on the boards, the warm sun beating down on me. But the boardwalk didn't seem to like me being so comfortable and began bucking again. It stopped when I got up on my knees. But by now my knees were sore and torn and wouldn't take much more of this. I tried leaning on my forearms — my left forearm and what was left of my right forearm — but after a while that got to be uncomfortable, too. So then I tried sitting on my ass, but the boardwalk didn't like that, either. That was like trying to sit on a bucking bronco, and pretty soon it bucked me right into the water.

I was sitting in water up to my chest and jumped to my feet. Scummy, brown things dripped off me, and I hoped they weren't harmful, but at least the lake didn't seem to mind my standing up. It felt good to stand up straight, but I was furious at the boardwalk. I grabbed the end of it with my one hand and began pulling off boards. They were half rotten and came off easily. I began beating the boardwalk with rotten boards till they disintegrated in my hand.

It felt good beating up on something for a change, but the boardwalk didn't seem to mind. It just rested there quietly, without protest. It was as if this is what it had wanted all along. Maybe it would've liked me to stomp on it violently while I was coming across, but in that case why did it let me only crawl on hand and knees? Maybe it just enjoyed watching my misery. It was used to being abused and only knew how to give abuse. But I wasn't about to hop back on and stomp on it to test my theory.

I soon got tired of beating it up, especially since it didn't react, and I turned around and started walking toward the shore. The bottom was level and solid but slippery, covered with slime. The water came just above my knees and didn't get any deeper. I used a rotten board to probe the bottom for hidden holes or weak spots ahead of me, but I didn't find any. Brown, scummy things swirled around me, making the bottom difficult to see through the shallow, murky water.

I must've walked miles, and my back was aching from bending over to probe with the rotten board. The brown, scummy things grew thick around me, and soon I was walking through sludge, but the bottom remained solid. By the time I reached shore, I was walking more on sludge than on the lake bottom. In fact, the shore was just more sludge, but drier and more compact. I kept walking inland, ankle deep in sludge, making slow progress.

"Nice trick," I said to the day. My voice sounded strange to my ears. "I couldn't have thought that one up in my worst nightmare." Or maybe I just did think it up, and this really was my worst nightmare. Or second worst, after my encounter with the dark woods. But then I remembered what the man had told me, the one I met in the street: if you think you're dreaming, you can't be dreaming, because if you're dreaming, you can't be thinking. Maybe I should just start thinking a little harder. But what if I thought as hard as I could and still didn't wake up? Maybe that would prove this was no dream. Or maybe it would prove I wasn't really thinking, but only dreaming I was thinking. The harder I thought about that the more confused I got. So what's the good of thinking? It was hard enough just trudging through all that sludge.

I must've trudged for hours, except the sun still stood at a little past noon. The plain of sludge seemed to extend forever to the horizon. But then clumps of stinging grass began appearing here and there. I wondered if the day's next trick was to pack so much stinging grass around me I'd be trapped again. Maybe I'd get another chance to try out the piece of glass, find out if the stinging grass would burn.

But that never happened. The stinging grass kept its distance, and the sludge gradually turned into solid ground. Just to be sure, I stooped down and scraped up some dirt in my one hand. The dirt was grainy with sand, and dry, but definitely good, brown dirt. I wondered if that was what the sludge was, grainy, brown dirt that got wet and bloated up. Maybe I shouldn't have been so repulsed by it. But the sludge floated in water while dirt would have settled to the bottom. Maybe the sand grains in the dirt were not really sand, but some kind of stuff that turned into a sticky, buoyant mass when it got wet, like the sludge. I should've looked at the sludge more closely when I was trudging through it, but I didn't want to turn back and find out now.

More vegetation began appearing around me, and not just stinging grass. In fact, the stinging grass gradually disappeared, and I can't say I was sorry about that. Now it was just ordinary-looking shrubs and plants and even a few wild flowers here and there. Not that I know anything about shrubs, plants and wild flowers, but these didn't look fake, not like the dark woods I saw back across the lake and the marsh. I even paused and sniffed one of the flowers, but of course I didn't smell anything. I hadn't smelled anything around here except that rotten stench.

And then I heard something. This was the first time since I came through the underpass that I heard anything other than the sound of my own voice, and my footsteps. I stopped and listened to the distant sound. A long, low, richly resonant, unwavering tone, a single, perfectly-pitched note that never stopped, played on some kind of wind instrument, except that nobody had that much breath. I had never in my life heard anything so beautiful. I shivered and almost wept listening to it. I wondered if that note had restored my hearing. Maybe it was a healing sound. Maybe it would cure me of all my other afflictions.

But of course it was a trap. A siren-sound. My first honey-trap of the afternoon, so to speak. They couldn't trap me in one of their ugly traps, so now they'd try something sweet.

"Who do you think you're kidding?" I said aloud to the day. My voice almost sounded normal. Of course, they would have to restore my hearing if their trap was going to work, whoever they were. Maybe that's what had happened. They had selectively taken away part of my hearing and most of my sense of smell. I wondered what else they'd taken away from me. Certainly not the sensation of pain, or hunger pangs, or thirst. I wished they'd taken those away instead. But maybe not. Everything hurts, only the last thing kills. So I should be grateful for the life I have, and the fact they keep reminding me I still have it. Maybe it's supposed to be our pain, our hunger, and our thirst that remind us we're still alive, in case we happen to forget.

I followed the sound for a long time. Through glades and groves, across meadows, and I finally found myself walking on a dirt track. It had wide, double ruts like a well-used jeep trail. I came to a crossing in the trail, paths running off to the left and the right, and the trail running straight ahead. And that's what it comes down to, isn't it? You can go left, right or straight ahead, go back where you came from, or stay where you are. Or cut across the unmarked countryside to be drowned in the bog, or stung to death by nettles, or lost in that wilderness forever. Maybe that's what they call free will. A lot of alternatives creating the illusion of choice.

But I'm always hopeful. So I went straight ahead, following the siren sound, which is what you would've done, too, isn't it? Whatever you are.

Then in a clearing I came upon a house and a barn. The barn sat on a low rise, the back of the barn overlooking a valley. A wide, gleaming river coiled through the valley. Those must've been the structures and valley and river I had seen from the mountainside. I wondered why I hadn't seen the marsh or the lake from there. And the relative positions of structures, valley, and river didn't seem quite right. It was as if, in preparation for my arrival, they had been hastily thrown together at the last minute, and the planner didn't quite get it according to the original plan I had seen from the mountainside.

The long, low note came from behind the barn, not much louder than when I first heard it, but seeming somehow much closer. I circled around to the end of the barn. Facing the valley and the river, a low platform ran the width of the barn. It looked like the stage I had seen at the strip mall, but nobody was on the stage behind the barn. The sound rose up from the stage, or maybe came out of the back wall of the barn, but I didn't see a source, nothing like a speaker, radio or phonograph. It was as if the musician had played that one note and then left the stage with his instrument, leaving the note behind to continue on its own.

I waited there listening to the delicious sound, waiting for the trap to spring, but nothing happened. Maybe it wasn't a trap at all. Maybe it was just a note that wanted to be listened to. I was happy to oblige, and glad I had got more of my hearing back. I wondered, if I walked far enough away from it, whether I'd lose most of my hearing again. Maybe that was the trick. It was bribing me with my hearing. Of course I didn't know if I really had all my hearing back. All I had heard so far was the sound of myself and that note.

I began wandering around the yard, looking for other people. I peeked inside the barn, which was empty: no animals, farming equipment, no hay in the hayloft. I headed down toward the house, a tidy, two-story building with a wide, covered porch. The long, low note followed me across the yard.

Maybe I'd finally get a decent glass of water, maybe even a bite to eat. I had almost reached the porch when I thought I saw someone coming around the corner of the building. I should've been glad to see a human face again, but for some reason I didn't want to look at this one. I climbed up on the porch and knocked on the door, and suddenly she was standing right next to me. I turned and looked at her, reluctantly. She was someone familiar, but I couldn't remember her name or what she had meant to me, even though I was certain I had known her for years.

I remembered she had once been pretty, a light sprinkle of freckles under green eyes, but now she looked bloated and haggard, the freckles had faded, her eyes were red, and she was angry.

"What did you do with the article?" she said. I think she said article. Or maybe she said something that simply made me think article, an article of clothing, a piece of merchandise, a written essay, a chapter of our nation's constitution. Something definitely hers, something she left deliberately vague, about which I knew nothing, and I knew she wasn't going to tell me what it was. I resented the accusation that I had somehow made off with it, whatever it was, or that she was trying to make me feel guilty about something I knew nothing about.

She said, "You treated me like an old hat."

"I thought you were dead." Hoping she would take the hint and crawl back to wherever she came from.

"In your dreams," she said.

"In my dreams you're alive and well right now — or maybe not so well, but alive."

"What makes you think you're dreaming?" she said.

"What makes you think I'm not?" I said. But that question had got me in a lot of trouble today, and I hoped we wouldn't get into it now, and I turned back to the door.

"You don't know, do you?" she said.

"Go blow your horn someplace else, baby." And then I thought, What a strange thing to say, and wondered where that line came from. I still saw her in the corner of my eye, but she was silent. Maybe my comment had shut her up. Just then the door opened.

"What took you so long?" the man said. He looked familiar, too, but I couldn't place him. I entered the house, and she followed me in, but the man ignored her. If she was a ghost, maybe he couldn't see her. Well, I'd pretend I didn't see her, either. But it bothered me I didn't know what article she was talking about. I almost wanted to ask her, but I was pretty sure she wouldn't tell me. Asking her would just make her angrier, as if she thought I was baiting her by pretending not to know.

The man said, "Welcome to the party."

"What's the occasion?"

"We're celebrating Moon Dog Day."

"What's that?"

"That's the last day of your life up to now."

"Up to now? That's every day. Every moment of every day of your life is a now at some time or other."

"Every day but the last up to now can't be Moon Dog Day, now, can it?"

He wasn't making any sense, so I decided to humor him. "So are you expecting a lot of moon dogs tonight?"

He turned around and shouted into the room, though I didn't see anyone there: "What do you think, guys, are we expecting a lot of moon dogs tonight? Because if there isn't..." He turned back to me. "It looks like they're not expecting much tonight. But then it looks like they're not *not* expecting much."

"How could it be Moon Dog Day if there's no moon dogs?"

"How could there be anything if there's nothing? How could there be nothing if there's not nothing? But somehow there always is, like it or not." I wasn't sure what to say, and he went on: "I heard you talking outside about dreaming."

"So you saw who I was talking to?" I said.

"Everyone you meet in a dream is just a version of yourself, but these — these are real people." He gestured to all the real people sitting around in the room. Somehow I hadn't noticed them at first. I thought he was just shouting into an empty room. Maybe the angry woman was still distracting me too much, even though I had decided not to pay attention to her. Maybe the man had conjured up all those real people when he pointed at them. "That's how you know you're not dreaming," he said. "It's when they're real people."

His voice had taken on a tone I didn't like. I still couldn't place his face. He wandered off. One of the real people got up and came toward me. She was the woman I had met in the strip mall, my dancing partner. Or I thought it was my dancing partner, but I wasn't sure I remembered her features correctly, and I couldn't remember what she'd been wearing.

She said, "What happened to you, I looked all over for you?" So I guess she was my dancing partner, a real person.

"Why didn't you wait for me?" I said.

"I looked back and saw your bike lying on the ground, but no you."

That wasn't quite how I remembered it, but I didn't say anything. In the corner of my eye I still saw the angry woman, and to piss her off even more I bent down and tried to kiss my dancing partner. She turned her face away, and my kiss landed somewhere on the side of her head, where I got a mouthful of hair. I don't know if she did that on purpose, or whether something had drawn her attention, and she had turned her head to look at it.

But I couldn't imagine what might've drawn her attention. All I saw was a roomful of real people not doing much of anything. It looked like a boring party. So much for Moon Dog Day, the last day of your life till now. Maybe they were just waiting for something to happen. Like this Now changing into another Now, an infinite line-up of Moon Dog Days.

Behind me I heard the angry woman snickering. Then someone else came up to me. I recognized the large woman in the bright, blue pants suit, the one I had met in the street long ago. Or maybe earlier this afternoon. Or maybe no time at all ago. She grabbed my right arm and held the necrotic stump up close to her face.

"You need to get this looked at," she said.

"Are you a doctor?" I said, annoyed at the interruption. She didn't say anything, but shoved the stump in her mouth and bit down hard on it and chewed off a piece. The tip of the stump was pretty rotten and came off easily, and I couldn't imagine it tasted very good. It didn't hurt, but I was too surprised to do anything but stand and watch her bite it off.

My dancing partner didn't seem to notice. Or maybe she was just pretending not to notice. She said, "You're all covered in mud." Real observant, this one.

I pulled myself away from the large woman in the bright, blue pants suit and said, "It's been a rough day."

"You must've taken the long way around. Good thing you didn't get lost in the woods. You don't want to get stuck in them. You'd never get out."

I wondered if maybe I hadn't got out, anyway, but even talking about those woods, if they were the same woods I saw back by the marsh, was starting to scare me, so I changed the subject.

"Where can I get a bite to eat around here?" I said. I felt like I'd had this conversation before, so maybe it was safe to talk about it.

"It's potluck, didn't you bring anything?"

"Potluck. Everybody always brings too much, there has to be some leftovers."

"I guess everybody thought the way you did and didn't bring anything."

To hide my disappointment, I changed the subject again. "Do you come here often?"

"I live here."

"I thought the guy I met at the front door lives here."

"That's my boyfriend."

"I thought I was your boyfriend."

Her boyfriend came up to us. He must've overheard us. He said, "Maybe that's how he knows he's not dreaming." He was laughing, but he didn't sound friendly. Maybe he was pissed I thought I was her boyfriend. Actually, I didn't really think that, but I had said it, anyway, just to see what would happen.

"So how *do* I know I'm not dreaming?" I said.

"How should I know how you know? Maybe you don't. Not my problem." And that's when I recognized him, the taller of the two student types I had met in the street today. Behind me the angry woman was snickering. I was so annoyed, I could've hit her, but she ducked out of sight when I turned around. I turned back to the boyfriend. I could've hit him, too, but just then my dancing partner grabbed my arm, the left arm, still sore from the stinging grass. I flinched, but if she noticed it she probably thought I was just surprised, and she tugged harder.

She said, "Come on, let me show you the house."

We went upstairs to the bedroom. The boyfriend and the angry woman stood side by side near the open door, watching us. I didn't notice they had followed us upstairs. We were sitting on the bed, my dancing partner and I, and she began taking off her blouse. That's the first time I noticed what she was wearing. A powder-blue long-sleeved blouse. It had a lot of buttons, and she was taking her time unbuttoning them. I kept looking at the two standing near the doorway.

She said, "Don't mind him, he likes to watch."

"What about her?"

"Get used to it."

She seemed annoyed I even asked. She kept on unbuttoning. Every button she unbuttoned seemed to reveal several more I hadn't noticed. One side of her blouse fell open, and I saw a little pink bud, stiff and erect, growing on one side of her chest. I got a huge hard-on looking at it, and reached out to touch it, but she snatched her blouse closed again. The angry woman standing at the door snickered, and I lost the hard-on.

My dancing partner kept unbuttoning the lower part of her blouse with one hand, and with her other hand she clenched the upper part closed. Then I noticed it was a long blouse. It descended past her knees, like a dress, and it had hundreds of buttons. With my one remaining hand, I grabbed her by the front of the blouse and was about to rip the whole thing open, when the boyfriend said in a threatening tone, "None of that."

I'd had enough of him and jumped up off the bed and launched myself at him. But he must've side-stepped me, or maybe he just faded away, and I plunged headfirst through the open doorway onto the landing outside. Maybe he wasn't really a real person. But the landing was crowded with real people. At first I thought the party had come upstairs to see what all the commotion was about, or what it was about to be about, but they didn't seem to be paying much attention to me. Or to anything going on in the bedroom. Or to much of anything at all.

I went back inside. The boyfriend and angry woman were no longer there. Maybe they had slipped outside when I wasn't looking, and had joined the real people on the landing, though I hadn't seen them there, either. My dancing partner had finally got her blouse off and was stretched out naked on the bed. I tried to close the bedroom door, but the floor must've been warped. The door only moved a few inches before it got stuck. I pulled on the door as hard as I could, and it made a cracking sound.

Someone outside said, "You break it, you buy it."

That got me really mad, and I got behind the door and began kicking it shut. It screeched across the floor a half-inch with every kick. Suddenly it swung free, banged against the door frame and fell off its hinges. I picked it up and leaned it against the doorframe and turned back to my dancing partner. But she was no longer stretched out naked on the bed. She had put on a tee shirt and a pair of jeans and was hanging up her long, powder-blue blouse in the closet.

"What's going on?" I said.

She turned to me and said, "Timing is everything." I wondered what time had to do with it, since I was pretty sure it was still a little past noon.

Then I noticed something else. The long, low note from behind the barn had stopped. It had gone on so long, I had stopped paying attention to it and only noticed its sudden absence. It must've stopped during all the racket I made kicking the door, because otherwise I would've noticed immediately it had stopped.

But maybe not. It could've stopped earlier, after I had walked in the front door and met all those real people and hadn't noticed when the long, low note had fallen silent. Then suddenly it occurred to me, it was the angry woman fussing at me on the front porch. That's when it must've stopped. She made it stop with all her fussing. Even noise must have a stop, just fuss at it long enough. In any case, I had got so used to the sound, the sudden silence was eerie.

I said to my dancing partner, "Do you hear that?"

"Hear what?"

"The silence," I said.

"You can't hear silence. There's nothing there to be heard."

"That sound, it's stopped."

"What sound?"

"Didn't you hear it?"

"All I ever hear is you. You never stop talking. How can anyone ever hear anything else?"

"I haven't been talking all that much. Didn't you just hear yourself talking? How about your boyfriend out there, he's definitely been talking."

"All I ever hear is you."

I shoved aside the unhinged door and we stepped out on the landing. The real people had vanished. I guess they all must've gone back downstairs when the entertainment ended. Well, not all of them. My dancing partner went ahead of me down the stairs, and I heard someone behind me. I turned around. The angry woman was standing at the head of the stairs, pounding her chest, wailing, "Here, here." I'm pretty sure that's what she meant, and not "Hear, hear," as if applauding, or demanding to be heard.

I said to my dancing partner, "What's up with her?"

"Just ignore her."

So I guess my dancing partner could see her, too, and the angry woman wasn't just a ghost only I could see. Nobody was downstairs. Maybe all the real people weren't all that real.

I said, "Where's the party?"

"Gone up to the barn, I guess."

"Well, let's go join them."

I hadn't noticed the angry woman was still behind me, till she grabbed my arm. For a ghost (if that's what she was), she had a pretty strong grip.

"You don't care, do you?" she said.

"Care about what?"

"You never cared."

"If I agreed would you shut up?"

"You don't care."

"I don't think you ever knew how much I did care," I said, "because you always wanted me not to care, so you'd have something to blame me for." I don't know how I knew all that. Just another memory flash, I guess. Or maybe something out of another movie I had seen somewhere. I pulled out of her grip and followed my dancing partner out the door.

My dancing partner didn't say anything, as if she hadn't even noticed. I tried to forget about the angry ghost and wondered what all those real people were doing up in the barn. Maybe trying to rev up that magical note again. But I didn't remember seeing anything in the barn that might do that.

I was about to say we should go up and join them, when I noticed my bike leaning against the porch. I would've noticed it when I came in the house, so someone must've put it there after I entered. She jumped down off the porch and straddled the bike.

"This time I drive," she said.

"What about the party?" I said.

"It's getting late."

Glancing up at the sky, I said, "It's only a little past noon."

"It's later than you think."

# ONE RASH WAD WAY IS SHY TIME

She held the bike steady while I hoisted myself on the handlebars. I was heavier than she was, but she pedaled off effortlessly. She must've been a strong cyclist, though she was just a slim slip of a girl. We coasted down the hill toward the river, following a double-rutted road like the jeep trail I came up on. From the looks of it, it should've been a bumpy ride but we seemed to be floating down, flying a few inches off the ground. But I wasn't sure, since the ground under the front wheel was going by in a blur, and I couldn't tell whether the tire was in contact with the ground.

We rounded a bend, and the trail ended at the edge of a bluff. I yelled for her to stop but she kept on pedaling and we sailed over the edge. It was a long drop, maybe twenty feet, and I thought the dream finally ends here. Or if it's not a dream — but we landed without a jolt at the foot of the bluff, by the riverside, so maybe the drop wasn't as long as I thought.

"How did you do that?" I said.

"Do what?"

"What you just did."

"What makes you think it was me?"

"You must've known we'd land safely."

"You must've known it, too."

"No, I didn't."

"Wait here," she said.

"Where are you going?"

"Don't go wandering off, I don't want to lose you again."

I was touched by this. Till now I had no idea what her feelings were. Now I thought she wants me, she needs me, maybe she's falling in love with me. Not that I know anything about falling in love. Love is a fine thing, or so I've heard, or at least I think I've heard, but I'm pretty sure I always knew that *falling* in love is a sickness, mostly afflicting adolescents and other emotional retards. I don't know how I know that. Survival instinct, I guess. I was perfectly happy if girls fell in love with me, as long as I was spared the disease of falling in love with them. Not that a lot of girls fell in love with me. In fact, I couldn't really remember if anybody had ever fallen in love with me. If they did, they never told me about it, not that I remember. Or maybe they told me about it, but I wasn't listening. But I think if someone had told me that, I would've been all ears. Maybe they told me, but I forgot. I seem to be forgetting a lot lately. I feel like I must've forgotten more this afternoon than I had ever learned in a lifetime.

I glanced up at the sky. It was only a little past noon. She disappeared into the bushes and I sat down next to the bike. The last time she disappeared, I had waited for her a long time, but this time I'd wait forever if necessary. Especially if she loved me. Someone who loves you is worth waiting for. Well, maybe not forever. But at least as long as I thought she loved me. Of course, the longer I waited, the less I would think that. If she was gone too long I'd stop thinking that altogether, especially if I had a hard time remembering things.

Then I began wondering why she said she didn't want to lose me again. As if she had owned me. As if I had been hers to lose.

All we did was dance around a bit and took a bike ride together. And then she had chosen me, I hadn't chosen her. She came up to me in the mall and dragged me off to dance with her, even when I hadn't really wanted to. At least that's how I remembered it. I sat on the sandy bank watching the river flow by, trying hard to remember everything that had happened. Not much of it really made sense, but by now I was almost used to that.

From where I sat, the river looked as wide as the wide, brown water I had waded across before I got to the farm. I saw hazy, low hills on the other side, miles away. But the water wasn't brown, it looked clean, deep and swift. I bent down and sniffed it, but I couldn't smell anything. I wondered if I dared to taste it. I cupped a few drops in my one hand and brought it to my lips. The water in my hand had a cool, gossamer feel, and didn't feel wet. My hand was dry when I touched my lips to it, to what I thought was the shiny sliver of water in my hand. I lowered my face to the river, which formed here a shallow, quiet little inlet. Bright sand gleamed on the bottom. Tiny, winged fish flitted about, and here and there luminous, yellow-green plants swayed in the eddy. I thought if those things could live there, the water was probably drinkable. I put my lips down on the surface but they didn't feel anything, and I buried my head deeper, almost to the bottom, and drank, but it was like sucking cool, dry air. I finally gave up and sat back on my heels. My head should have been dripping wet, but it was completely dry.

I wanted my dancing partner to return and show me what to do. She lived in the area and she should know where to get a drink of water. If she led me to drinkable water I'd really fall in love with her, for the first time in my life I'd really fall in love with someone, I'd love her forever, I'd cherish her unto eternity. Or at least I'd make an effort to fake it.

I went on like this for a long time, making as many promises as I could think of. With practice it became more and more easy to make them. I made them aloud to anything that might listen, or to anything that might not, to the shrubbery nearby, to the tiny, winged fish in the river, to the air. At first I stammered, since I wasn't used to saying such things, but then the words flowed fluently from my mouth, as cool and airy as the river. I must've made hundreds of promises, maybe thousands. In the end, after hours or days, I had made so many promises that I could hardly remember a single one. Fortunately my dancing partner turned up before I could make so many that I'd forget all of them. She came around a bend in the river in a rowboat and beached the rowboat in the sand where I sat.

She jumped out and said, "You haven't been drinking the water, have you?"

"I couldn't."

"That's good."

"What's wrong with this water?"

"Don't drink it, that's what's wrong with it."

"I'm dying of thirst, I really need some water."

"Fine, just don't drink this."

I gave up trying to get anything more out of her. I wondered, if I had remembered more of my promises, whether she would've been more forthcoming. But how could she know whether I remembered my promises or not? Especially as I never had a chance to break any. Maybe she knew by the way everybody here but me seemed to know everything about me.

I said, "Where'd you get the boat?"

She nodded upriver: "From the landing."

"That landing must be a long ways off. I've been sitting here forever."

"It's just around the bend."

I thought that bend must bend half-way around the world but I didn't say anything. I was beginning to think that not everybody's sense of time is the same as mine. If we both had watches, we could synchronize them and then compare the times later and find out how different our senses were. But I wasn't sure that would work, either. Maybe different clocks measured time differently. Around here you could never be too sure.

She picked up the bicycle and dropped it in the prow of the boat. She pulled the boat off the sand and swung the prow around to point at the river.

"Get in," she said. She sounded impatient. I waded in the water and started to step in over the side. "Aft, aft." I guess that meant I should climb in the rear. She got in and sat down in the middle facing me. She said, "You're not getting an oar, I want to be sure we go straight with the current." She spoke with forced patience, as if she were talking to an annoying child.

"What's downriver?" I said.

"Water."

I wondered if she meant real water or more of this dry, airy stuff. If by rain she didn't mean the same thing I did, then maybe by water she didn't mean the same thing, either.

The thought of real water downriver made me hopeful. But I didn't ask her if it was really real. I was pretty sure I wouldn't get a straight answer. She unshipped the oars and pulled on them, and immediately the current gripped us. She must've been as good at rowing as she was at cycling. Hardly ever looking over her shoulder, she seemed to know exactly where she was going. The river surged and swished alongside us but she kept a steady course. The land receded from us, but the far shore didn't seem to get any closer. So far out on the water, I started to feel panicky, but then I thought it probably wouldn't matter if I fell in. I could probably breathe it if I had to. I wondered why we were navigating so far from land.

She said, "No snags or eddies out here."

I didn't remember asking her. Maybe by now she knew me well enough to know everything I wanted to ask her. It was humiliating to be thought so predictable. I must be a boring person. I don't know why she bothered with me. Why she was taking so much trouble to carry me off to wherever. And wouldn't even condescend to tell me where. By now all my promises of love for her seemed stupid and irrelevant. I was embarrassed thinking about them.

In fact, I was beginning to hate her. I thought of all the meaningless and evasive answers she had given me, and if my one hand hadn't been clutching a gunwale so tightly I would've got up then and there and kicked her cock-teasing ass overboard. Except she was pretty strong. She'd probably kick mine before I got anywhere near her. And do it without capsizing the boat.

A mist rose up from the water and the land disappeared from view. The sun burned down through the mist, a flowing, luminous veil overhead. The water was deep and clear. Tiny, winged fish flitted about near the surface, and every now and then larger, winged fish rose from the depths and snapped them up. Once a massive, winged fish, nearly the length of the boat, came up and nudged the hull. The big fish was dark, pulsating gold, streaks of green and mauve running along its back. The boat lurched and swayed but the big fish soon lost interest and flung itself back into the deep. I guess anything that floated through that airy stuff needed wings. I wondered how that stuff could support our weight on the surface. Maybe it repelled weighty things and only took in things with wings, as airy as itself.

Maybe it would support my weight if I fell in. But falling in didn't seem like such a good idea. Even if I had wings like the winged fish, they'd probably make an exception in my case, whoever they were, whatever was running things around here. With my luck I'd probably sink straight to the bottom, no matter how hard I tried to stay afloat. I couldn't see the bottom but, judging from the size of the big fish as it plunged on down, I could see over a hundred feet below. Below that, the deep disappeared in a brilliant, blue-green fog. Maybe here the river had no bottom, like my dream, if it was a dream.

The mist thickened, and soon I could hardly see the prow of the boat. Sunlight scattered through the mist and the air was burning white. Every now and then, brilliant rainbow colors shot through the heavy air and faded away. The current had slowed. In fact, the water alongside was flat as glass, and I could hardly tell we were moving, except from the slow creak of the oarlocks as she pulled on the oars.

She said, "Can you row?"

"Never done it. You never let me."

"You should learn."

"I thought I wasn't getting an oar."

"That was back then." I wanted to ask her what was the big difference between now and back then, when the mist suddenly thickened and formed a brilliant, white shroud around her. I heard her say inside the cloud, "Better sooner than later."

We drifted for a while. The creaking of oarlocks had stopped.

"Do you want me to take over now?" I said, but she didn't say anything. The mist thinned a little and I saw she was no longer sitting there. I was alone in the boat. Me and the bicycle. I guess she had slipped overboard. Or maybe the white cloud had wafted her away. Maybe she was one of those airy things, too. Maybe that's why she seemed so light when I was pedaling the bike out of the mall, even though she seemed pretty solid when I held her at the dance. Maybe I should jump in after her and take the bike with me. I would meet her at the river bottom and we would ride together along the bottom till we reached land. If there was a bottom, if there was land. I wasn't sure there was, and that might've been the only reason I didn't jump in. That and the fact that the idea terrified me. Besides, she had practically told me I should row now.

I crawled forward and took her place in the middle, but then I wondered how I was going to row with only one hand. But when I touched an oar, it suddenly sprang to life. It seemed to move on its own, guiding my hand with its movements. Of course, even I knew that if you keep pulling on just one oar the boat will go in circles. But then I noticed the other oar was moving, too, without my touching it. When I lifted my hand off the left oar, they both stopped moving. And then they started moving again when I touched it.

I guess they somehow must've been joined mechanically by some device under the keel. So she was just faking her rowing skills all along. She probably didn't know the first thing about rowing. I wondered what would happen if I sat facing the other way and grasped the other oar. Maybe I'd start moving backwards against the current, if there still was a current. But I was in no mood to experiment.

Gradually the mist thinned and sometimes I could see land miles away. I started to miss her, to regret the mean things I had thought about her. I wondered if that's why she left me. But then I imagined her turning up again and saying in her snippy voice, What happened to you, I looked all around for you. As if I had abandoned her and not the other way around. This time there was no excuse, no way I could have abandoned her. I started feeling resentful again. The bitch had been jerking me around since the minute I met her. I just couldn't figure out why. What was in it for her? Maybe there was no reason. Why does everything have to have a reason? Maybe sometimes things just happen. Maybe she wasn't even aware of what she was doing, and with that thought I started to miss her again.

# WHY EOS RAT DIES IN SHAM WAY

The mist had mostly cleared, but here and there it hung in gauzy, white shrouds over the water, barely moving. The boat started drifting through a cloud, and I tried manipulating the oars to navigate around it. But the oars ignored me, and the boat kept on going through the cloud. It seemed like hours before I came out on the other side. Dead ahead I saw land: a wide sandy shore, dunes, and beyond the dunes the tiled roofs of buildings, and half-naked people, or more like nine-tenths naked, sunbathing in the sand.

The oars quickly picked up speed, creating a lot of froth in the boat's wake. It's as if the boat had got excited on approaching land. Of course that's silly. A boat can't get excited, it's just a boat. Its hidden machinery must've been programmed to speed up when it detected land. The boat hit the beach with such force it slid its whole length on dry land before stopping, and nearly pitched me into the sand.

I got out and tried to shove it back in the water but it wouldn't budge. I guess it had come as far as it wanted and had no intention of going backwards. Maybe the boat had a will of its own. But that was silly, too. A hollow, wooden thing can't have a will of its own, at most it was a machine. I tried turning it over to see what was underneath, but it still wouldn't budge. It's as if it suddenly weighed a ton, and I guess it was going to keep its secrets to itself.

I picked up the bike, hoisting it on my shoulder to keep sand off the chain and sprockets. At least the bike wasn't heavy. In fact, it was so light I barely felt its weight and I wondered why it had seemed so heavy when I rode it along the embankment outside the strip mall. Maybe here gravity, like time, changes with the whims of whoever's running the show.

I climbed up a dune past a couple of sunbathers, who ignored me. On the other side of the dune, stone steps led up to a broad esplanade. I climbed the steps and set the bike down on the pavement. A few bikers went by, and some strollers. The people were all young and good-looking. Tall, big-eyed, broad-shouldered young men with wide, dimpled jaws and easy, confident gaits. Flaxen-haired, dewy-eyed, dark-eyed, green-eyed, tawny-skinned, curvy, slim young women. Wasp-waisted, bug-eyed, bosomy blond girls with cupid-bow mouths and plushy lips.

A lot of them wore spotless white sweats bearing the same black logo on the front. I couldn't quite make out the logo, since the words were partly covered up, or the person turned away just as I started to read it. But eventually I made out the letters NIV, and beneath them the word OF, and something else below that, so I guess the logo referred to a uNIVersity OF something or other. I guess I must've wandered a long way from home, since I don't remember a uNIVersity anywhere near the town. I leaned the bike against the parapet of the esplanade and went up to one of the young men.

"Where can I find a water fountain around here?" I said.

"Sorry, dude," he said without stopping, "I'm totally tapped out." Did the fool think I was asking for money? Or maybe he thought I thought he was a water fountain. In that case, why didn't he just tell me he was not a water fountain? Not that I didn't already know.

"Water," I shouted after him, "where can I find water?" Without turning he made a lazy, dismissive gesture with his hand and kept on walking.

I got on the bike and pedaled past a news rack, headline clearly displayed: WHY EOS RAT DIES IN SHAM WAY. Not an inch of spray paint covering it. I guess the people here were a lot neater than they were downtown, but I didn't stop to figure out what the headline meant, and I kept on toward the tile-roofed buildings. They were five-, six- and seven-story buildings, all a sandy, beige color, clustered around sloping, immaculate lawns of such intense green I hardly believed the grass was real. I was about to get off the bike and examine the grass more closely, when a shadow passed overhead.

I looked up and, for the first time since I walked through the underpass, I saw a cloud in the sky. It was not like the clouds downtown that flitted by so briskly they must've been fast-forwarded. This cloud billowed along the sky, massive and slow, heading toward the river, followed by other clouds. Soon the sky was covered with them, and a chilly breeze sprang up.

I was riding along a broad path of sand-colored flagstones, when a man on a motorized tricycle overtook me and shouted at me to stop. He was wearing a sandy, beige uniform and service cap with a polished bill.

He said, "Walk your bike on the walkway." He sounded angry.

"Sorry," I said, and got off the bike. "Is there a drinking fountain around here?"

"What did you call me?"

"A drinking fountain. Is there — ?"

"I had it up to here with you smart-ass punks."

Not knowing what smart-ass punks he meant, I didn't say anything, which was probably the wrong answer. He got off his tricycle and grabbed the bike from me. He lifted it up in the air and smashed it down on the flagstones. A few pieces broke off. He lifted it up again and smashed it repeatedly on the flagstones till the wheels were bent and bowed. He tossed the ruined bike onto the lawn.

He said, "Now look what you did." But he no longer sounded so angry. In fact, he sounded somewhat sheepish. "Next time, that's a sight." Or maybe he meant cite. I'm pretty sure he didn't mean site. If he did I would've been even more confused.

He got back on his tricycle and drove off. I didn't see how there could be a next time, since my bike was no longer rideable. But I was too surprised to say anything about it, which was just as well.

A dark cloud lumbered by above, trailing a blue emptiness in the sky, which another cloud swallowed up. The sky was turning black, and I was shivering with cold. I had left home in khakis and tee shirt and wasn't prepared for the sudden change in weather. I made for the nearest building to get in out of the cold. I pulled on the double glass door, but it was locked.

Through the glass I saw an old man standing inside looking out, but then I realized I was looking at my own reflection. He was covered in dried mud, thin, bent and bowed like the wheels of my bicycle after the tricycle man had pounded them on flagstones. In the chilly breeze, thin wisps of white hair floated over his balding head, his right forearm rotting off. I should've been shocked. I was a young man when I left home. Or at least a man of early middle age. But maybe I wasn't all that young when I left home. Maybe I only left home with the illusion that I was a young man. But somehow I wasn't shocked. Instead I felt a crushing sense of shame. This is what I had come to, this is what I had always been. I must've been like this forever, thinking I was like these beautiful, entitled, young people walking around me, and never knowing how ridiculous I must've seemed to them, a doddering old popinjay. Fool that too late repents, age is unnecessary, being weak seem so. I don't know where those words came from, they just popped into my head. I don't even know what they mean. They can't have come out of nowhere, they must've come out of something I had read, and then forgotten.

The cold had grown intense and snowflakes swirled in the air. Now I knew I could not only feel hunger, thirst, pain, and shame, but I could also feel cold. I was almost starting to feel human again.

The old man on the other side of the glass tried shoving the door open for me, but it stayed closed. I suppose the two of us could've cracked open that door, but I didn't want the tricycle man coming around again. Next time is a cite, I decided he'd said. Cop talk for citation, I guess. If he meant citation, why didn't he just say so? I hardly knew what citation meant, either. Something worse than getting my bike smashed, I guess.

I turned away from the glass door. In the corner of my eye I saw the old man behind the door turn away, too. He'd probably given up on me and was going farther into the building. Then I remembered he was just my reflection. I wondered why I kept forgetting that. Maybe the shame of him being me was too much to put up with on an afternoon like this.

I guess it was still a little past noon. But the clouds had swallowed up the sun, and my shadow along with it. I could no longer tell the time or the direction I was going in. It was worse than downtown. The sky had grown dark and snowflakes whipped around me. Two men came out of a building nearby and I hurried toward them to reach the door before it swung shut. One of them waved at me and the other turned back into the building. I thought for sure they were going to close me out but the one who had waved held the door open for me. He smiled and clapped me lightly on the shoulder as I passed him, and of course

I instantly suspected another trap. I thought I'd punch him in the face and get it over with once for all, but he said, "You must be freezing, come on in and get warmed up."

His expression was so kind, his voice so gentle, I almost wept, even while I still half doubted his sincerity. I followed him down a hallway into a large room full of people. A fire burned in a fireplace at one end. Tall, arched windows overlooked the sloping lawns outside, now covered with snow. The people sat around on wide sofas, holding cups of steaming liquid and chatting among themselves. Maybe my tormentors (whoever they were) were staging a repeat performance of my dancing partner's Moon Dog Day party back at the farm, with variations. Most of the people were older than the youngsters walking around outside, but they all looked well-dressed, fit and cheerful. I passed a group who seemed to be talking about some author, I didn't catch which one.

"I think I preferred *When the Sun Still Stood*," said one.

"You mean *Stood Still*."

"No, it's definitely *Still Stood*."

"I can see how the sun could seem to stand still — wasn't that in the Bible someplace? — but what does it mean to say it still stands?"

"Didn't Nietzsche say the eternal recurrence begins at noon?"

"Who?"

"Nietzsche. I know you know who Nietzsche is. Or if you don't, I hope you're too ashamed to admit it."

"Oh. I thought you said, 'Need she say the eternal recurrence begins at noon?' I was wondering who that 'she' was, and why she would need to say such a thing."

"You must've heard me say 'didn't' before I mentioned Nietzsche."

" 'Didn't need she say?' That doesn't make any sense."

The conversation lapsed a moment, then one said: "I heard he was in a coma."

"Nietzsche?"

"He still is," said another. "Been that way for months — fully conscious but locked in, apparently."

"Sounds like my brother-in-law doing ten to twenty. Except I'm not sure my brother-in-law is fully conscious."

"Well, at least he should know by now if it's standing still or still standing." And they all laughed. It sounded like the punchline of a dirty joke, but whatever the joke was, I didn't get it. Maybe each of them laughed because everybody else laughed, but privately none of them got the joke, either.

Then one of them said, as if returning to the topic they had been discussing before I walked in, "The quality of the dreaming experience is fundamentally different from that of the waking experience, in ways that are impossible to explain, but obvious to almost everyone."

"*Almost* everyone?" said one. "So who is it not obvious to?"

"Psychotics, retards and small children?" said another.

"Now there's a farcical, facetious fellow," said another.

"In a dream," said the dream expert, "it's impossible to ask if you're dreaming and at the same time to expect an intelligible answer."

"Then we're all dreaming," said the farcical, facetious fellow.

"We can't all be dreaming the same dream at the same time, can we?"

"Well, if we aren't then whose dream is this, anyway?"

My shame returned when I imagined what a sad spectacle I presented to the room. I would've turned and fled, but a woman stood up and held out her hand to me. It was her left hand, which I could easily grasp without the awkward wrist twist I'd have performed if she had held out her right hand. She had a sweet, round face, tiny wrinkles in the corners of her eyes, and she never stopped smiling.

She said, "I'm so glad I finally met you, I've heard so much about you."

I searched her face for signs of irony or ridicule, but only saw a gentle face, open and smiling. A face eager to be accepted and enjoyed, and which I had no recollection of ever having seen before.

I said, "You're mistaking me for someone else."

She broke into a soft laugh and hooked her arm through mine and led me toward the fire. I wondered when the trap would spring. Of course it only sprang when I least expected it, so maybe if I kept expecting it I could delay it for a while.

A couple got up from a couch near the fire and offered us their seats. Somebody handed me a steaming cup. It looked like hot cocoa with a delicate swirl of thick cream on top. To my surprise it smelled sweet. I hadn't smelled anything sweet since I left home. Maybe I had never smelled anything sweet, even at home. I couldn't remember what I had smelled at home, if anything, but I must've smelled something sweet at one time or another, otherwise how would I know what sweet smelled like?

I brought the cup to my lips and stuck my tongue in the liquid but it was too hot to taste. Maybe that was the trick. Tantalize me with sweet smells and then burn my tongue off. Still the cup was not too hot to hold and I liked to feel its warmth in my one hand.

She said, "I attended your lecture last week, absolutely the most fascinating thing I've heard in years, it completely blew me away."

I wondered how to show her that I had no idea what she was talking about and that I knew she didn't, either, and she couldn't have attended a lecture I delivered, since I knew I had never delivered any. Now that I think about it, I'm not sure how I knew that. But I'm pretty sure I did know.

Remembering the newspaper headline I had seen outside, I said, "I've had to revise my original conclusions since eos rat died in sham way."

Without blinking she placed a hand on my necrotic arm and said, "I know, that was such a shame, but in my opinion that can only strengthen your original conclusions."

Someone said, "Who is Eos?"

"The mythical goddess of dawn," someone else said.

"Why would they name a rat after her?"

"They didn't," said someone. "E.O.S. means Emergency Operating System, R.A.T. means Regressive Analysis Tool."

"E.O.S. means Energy Optimization State," someone else said.

My companion whispered to me, "I just love it when the computer guys and the physicists get into it."

"But sham way means they died inauthentically, whatever they are," said someone.

Someone else said, "I thought Sham Way was the street where it happened." But nobody paid attention to him.

The kind man who had let me in the front door came up to us and stood by the couch, listening. Then he said, "Whatever they are, an inauthentic death still has to be *authentically* inauthentic if it's genuinely sham."

A half dozen others had gathered around us, and I heard a gentle murmur of assent, till my companion said, "And conversely an authentic death can be *inauthentically* authentic."

They went on like this for a while, till they had exhausted every possible combination of authentic and inauthentic, and the kind man concluded thoughtfully, "Yes, that all does make sense."

My companion touched my knee and said, "Of course, your evidence also allows for the fact it makes sense." Then raising her eyebrows hopefully at me, "Doesn't it?"

I said, "I guess it allows for anything you want." A sigh of relief seemed to pass around the room, and some people began quietly clapping. The kind man patted me on the shoulder and my companion stroked my necrotic arm. Then the crowd fell silent and made way for a portly man in a brown corduroy jacket. He seemed like someone who commanded at least as much respect as I did, and suddenly I began to feel jealous. Gray hair girded his bald crown. Reflected in the thick lenses of his glasses, snowflakes batted against the windows behind me. He stood before me silently a moment, holding an unlit pipe. Then he stuck the pipe in his mouth and nodded.

Then he removed the pipe and said, "On the one hand..."

And stuck the pipe back in his mouth and sucked on it loudly. I expected him to say more but he remained silent. An ambiguous murmur passed around the crowd and someone laughed quietly. Then I saw he was staring at my necrotic arm and I wondered if he was referring to my missing hand. I couldn't see anything funny in just saying, "On the one hand." But maybe he was making some kind of inside joke only his audience could understand. I was about to jump up and shove that pipe down his throat. Let's see how funny that is.

But then I thought maybe he wasn't looking at my necrotic arm at all. His thick lenses obscured which way his eyes were turned. I could only see the blizzard outside reflected on his glasses. He could've been looking at something else entirely, so I relaxed on the couch and brought the hot cup to my mouth again.

It was still too hot to taste. So far this cup of hot cocoa (if that's what it was) was the only joke I had met so far. Maybe it would always be too hot to taste, no matter how long I held it in my hand. Maybe that was supposed to be the joke, the one I found so unfunny and everyone else hilarious.

My companion said, "So cozy sitting by the fire on a snowy afternoon." To my surprise she leaned her head on my shoulder. I set the mug of hot cocoa (if that's what it was) down on the floor beside the couch and began stroking her knee with my one remaining hand. I wondered how far up her thigh I could stroke before she stopped pretending not to notice.

The crowd murmured, "True, true, so true."

The portly man took the pipe from his mouth and nodded. I expected him to say something else but then he put the pipe back in his mouth.

On an impulse I lifted my hand from her knee and said loudly, "But on the other hand..." Gales of laughter shook the room. The portly man took the pipe out of his mouth and smiled. Then he put the pipe back in his mouth and sucked on it so loudly it sounded like a toilet flushing.

Then he took the pipe out and said, "But getting back to my main point."

And put the pipe back in his mouth. His comment only produced a general titter in the room, and a few chuckles. The portly man frowned and bit down on the pipe stem so hard I heard it crack.

I raised my necrotic arm and said, "And then again on the one hand."

The roars of laughter went on for a long time. At times the laughter seemed about to die down, but then someone would raise an arm and say, "And on the other hand," and the laughter started up again. The portly man flushed purple and the veins in his head seemed about to burst. He turned around and stomped out of the room, slamming the door. A few derisory hoots followed him out.

My companion said, "I just love it when you two get into it."

I said, "I guess I won this round, didn't I?"

She looked at me, her brow furrowing. "Win? What round? What are you talking about?"

I said, "You know, dueling wits, stuff like that."

She said, "To me, it's about the interactive, interpersonal nature of truth, which can only be discovered by the give and take of intelligent minds."

I raised my necrotic arm and said, "But on the other hand." She just stared at me. The crowd had drifted away, and nobody was laughing.

I said, "I guess I must not be one of those intelligent minds."

She pulled away from me. "Who are you, anyway?"

"I was hoping you'd tell me," I said.

She stood up. "If you don't know, how do you expect me to?"

I said, "For a moment back then I thought you did know."

She said, "I thought I did, too."

She seemed about to walk away, but the kind man, who had drifted away, was drifting back. He said, "But does anybody really know who they really are?"

She seemed to think about that a moment and sat down again. "You're right, I apologize, I misunderstood you, you're testing us, aren't you? it's just a test."

The kind man said, "This is a genuinely wise and humble human being." I wasn't sure if he was talking about me or her, or maybe himself, since he was gently patting his chest as he spoke. Then he began speaking quietly, as if to himself, but loudly enough for everyone to hear him. I wasn't sure what he was talking about, but everyone listened attentively. He paced slowly back and forth in front of the fireplace, and from time to time he paused, drew breath, and slapped himself violently across both cheeks, first with one hand then the other, which I thought was pretty strange, but no one else seemed to think it was out of the ordinary.

The crowd had drifted back and soon everybody in the whole room had gathered around us. I heard the door opening and closing as others entered the room. Word must be spreading all over the NIV what was going on here now.

The kind man fell silent and my companion said, "I am such a fool," and buried her face in her hands.

I said, "So now maybe you can tell me who I am?"

The kind man suddenly chortled. "Listen up, people, he's telling us only fools can tell us who we really are." An awed silence fell over the group.

I said, "Actually, what I really want to know is how to get home."

She raised her head. "If I hadn't known better, I'd have said: If *you* don't know...but you do know, don't you?"

I said, "No, I don't, but I'm still hoping someone does."

The kind man nodded gravely. "In other words, some questions cannot be answered. Some questions seem to make sense, but don't, and a question that seems to make sense when it doesn't make sense cannot yield to an answer that makes sense."

Someone said, "Some questions logically preclude the possibility of an answer."

Someone else said, "But if there's no possible answer, then there's no problem."

Another said, "What if the number of problems exceeds the number of possible answers?"

She jumped up and spread her arms. "He just wants to know the way home."

The kind man nodded again. "That brings it all back down to earth, yes, it's so easy to get lost in a rarified realm of abstraction."

She said, "But what does home mean?"

I heard various answers rise from the crowd.

"It's where the heart is."

"It's where you keep tomorrow's breakfast."

"It's where you keep all your books and rejected manuscripts."

"It's where you worry about the plumbing."

"It's where you don't need to worry about anything."

"Then the only true home has to be the grave."

I heard a lot of wheres but no directions how to get there. Somebody said, "All you need to know is what the next step is going to be."

The kind man, who was looking gloomy, suddenly brightened. "Of course, and then the step after that."

"And the step after that step," said someone else.

"And the step after the step after that step," said another.

The kind man said, "But on second thought, how can you know what step to take if you don't already know where you're going?"

"That was the second thought, what was the first thought?" someone said. He laughed at his own quip, but no one paid attention to him.

My companion said, "Does anybody really know where they're going?"

"True," the kind man said, "but that shouldn't prevent us from taking a step."

"And the step after that," said someone.

"And the step after the step after that," said someone else.

My companion said, "It's the journey, not the destination."

The kind man said, "Maybe that's what we do best — taking steps and never knowing where they lead."

"You're hardly one to talk," said someone. "You never stepped off campus in thirty years."

The kind man drew himself up and looked around the group. He said, "Every step I've ever taken has been an exploration and sometimes a discovery."

"That's true," someone said. "On any finite plane there are infinitely many steps that can be taken. There's no end to possible new discoveries."

Someone said, "But the finite plane needs to be larger than your foot, so you have room to step around in."

"Actually, larger than both feet," said someone else.

Someone else said, "Yes, and not all of the steps are going to be relevant."

"Define relevance," said someone.

My companion said, "The first thing you have to ask yourself is, Where am I? What time is it? And relevance has nothing to do with any of that."

The kind man nodded thoughtfully. "Relevance is irrelevant."

Someone said, "Well, good thing we always know what time it is, at least."

Someone else said, "So what time is it?"

They all looked at each other, but no one said anything. Then they looked at me.

"I'm guessing a little past noon," I said.

"A little past noon!" said my companion, jumping up.

The kind man looked at me apologetically. "Sorry, we're running a little late, I wish we had more time, this discussion has been a truly transformative experience for me."

My companion said, "We have to be there at half-past."

A thin, young man pushed forward with an annoyed expression on his face. He was wearing glasses and I could actually see his eyes through them. The glasses made his eyes look as tiny as two blue dots, as if the dots had been daubed on his face with the tip of a paint brush.

"But there's still time to hear my poem," he said.

The kind man looked doubtful. "I don't know — "

"I was scheduled to read at noon!" said the young man, his voice trembling with rage.

Someone said, "Read it and be quick about it."

But already people were drifting away. I heard the door opening and closing as some of the crowd were making their escape. The poet dug a piece of paper out of his pants pocket and unfolded it. The paper was limp and ragged, like an old wash cloth. By the time he'd finished unfolding it, it was more like a damp bath towel. I caught a glimpse of his handwriting, which was large, loopy and barely legible. The room was now half-empty. But my companion sat down beside me again, and impatiently drummed her fingers on her knee. The kind man stood there looking worried, shifting from foot to foot. I picked up the cup of hot cocoa, if that's what it was, and stuck my tongue in it but it was still too hot to taste. I set the cup back down on the floor beside the couch.

In a high, quavering monotone the thin, young man chanted, "You ever wanted to be a tree? I never wanted to be a tree, standing there year after year, my roots rotting out from under me, till one day, in a blustery wind, I fall over from the exhaustion of standing there doing nothing all those years except throwing shadows on the dirt when it shines, or dripping in the mud when it rains. Is that what you want to be? A goddam tree?"

The poet stopped and drew a shaky breath.

The kind man murmured, "Very nice. I like how it rhymes at the end."

But my companion jumped up and clutched my shoulder. "We've got to go."

The poet aimed the two blue dots of his eyes at me and said, "What do you think?"

I said, "It reminds me of my life."

My companion whispered in my ear, "Don't encourage him."

But it was true. Not that I remembered much about my life. But I found something ghastly about the young man's poem, as if something in it had once happened to me, though I couldn't remember what. Which made it all the more ghastly. His face broke into a lopsided smile, which I guess must've been a smile of gratitude. Or rather, the lower half of his face smiled, showing crooked, gray teeth, but the two blue dots of his eyes didn't change. So maybe it wasn't gratitude but I hate to think what it might've been. Standing up, putting her hand under the armpit of my rotting arm, my companion tugged me to my feet.

"Where are we going?" I said.

"Just next door."

We followed the rest of the crowd out the room and down the hall. We entered a large classroom filled with rows of little desks. They had sloping lids of ink-stained wood carved with ancient, blackened initials. Most of the desks were already occupied.

"Why are we here?" I said and turned around, but my companion and the kind man had disappeared. I found an empty desk at the front of the room. At first it seemed too small for me but after a while I got used to it, as if I had been sitting there my whole life. I lifted the lid of the desk and looked inside. It contained a large, glossy magazine, its pages torn, brittle and wrinkled with age. The magazine looked familiar, but I couldn't remember where I'd seen it before. I took it out and flipped through it. It was full of photographs of handsome young men and women modeling the hair and clothing styles of a half-century ago. I tried reading some of the captions, but the letters kept changing shape just when I was about to make out what the words meant.

The large woman in the bright, blue pants suit entered the room. For some reason, I wasn't surprised to see her. Or maybe for no reason at all, I wasn't surprise to see her. She was holding a stack of pamphlets and began handing out clumps of them to the head of each row. She handed me a clump, pretending not to recognize me.

She said to the class, "Do not open the test booklets till I say so."

I opened mine, but every page was blank.

She said, "Do not write in your test booklet, you will have eighty-five minutes in which to complete your essay questions, when I say time you will immediately put down your pencil, close your test booklets and insert your essays between the pages of your booklet, and you will write your names on the cover."

I said, "What essay questions?"

Nobody answered. I turned around and said to the kid behind me, "Let me borrow your pencil." He looked like a nine-year-old version of the poet. His mouth was frozen in a thin grimace of terror, but behind the lenses of his glasses the two blue dots of his eyes didn't change. At first I thought he was frightened of taking the test, then I realized he was frightened of me. I don't know how I knew that. Maybe he just looked like a kid who could easily pass tests but was terrified of people. He shook his head slightly and said something like, You're supposed to bring your own pencil. But it was hard to make out what he was saying through that thin grimace. I said, "Give me a fucking pencil or I'll bust every fucking four-eyes in your face."

"If you think I got four eyes you're the one needs glasses," he said. I admired his courage talking back to me like that, and I guess he'd grow up to be a great poet someday. But in the mean time I needed a pencil and grabbed the one he clenched in his hand. He looked helplessly at the woman in the blue pants suit, who ignored us, but he didn't say anything. I turned around and began writing in the margins and white spaces of the magazine. I'm not sure what I was writing about, maybe nothing, which is a hard subject to write about, but in any case I wrote about it quickly.

I had filled up almost every available space when the woman in the bright, blue pants suit said, "You may now open your test booklets." It was probably a good thing I started early because a moment later she said, "Time."

That was the shortest eighty-five minutes I had ever taken a test in. I tried rereading my essay. It didn't make much sense. I had filled in the widest white spaces first and then jumped around to the thinner spaces as I began running out of room. The magazine pages were glossy and the pencil had made a faint impression, hard to read. Since my writing hand had fallen off, my untrained left hand could only form large, nearly formless fourth-grade letters.

The woman said, "Pass your booklets up to the head of your row."

I inserted the magazine between the pages of the test booklet and turned around to give his pencil back to the kid, but his desk was empty. In fact, all the desks in the room but mine and hers were empty. The woman must've dismissed the class when I wasn't paying attention. Or maybe the school bell rang and I didn't hear it. The woman came to my desk and collected my test booklet.

"Where is everybody?" I said. She didn't answer but went back to her desk at the front of the classroom. She sat down and began reading through my magazine essay, marking passages with a red pencil.

After a while she looked up and said, "Your thoughts are still a little disorganized, but it's nicely illustrated."

I got up and went to her desk. "Why are we here?" I said. "What are we doing here?"

She looked at my right arm as if seeing it for the first time. "You really need to get that looked at."

She reached out as if to take hold of my arm, but I backed away. "Not another bite," I yelled. She reached for a note pad and began writing on it with her red pencil. She tore it off, folded it and held it out to me.

"Take this to the nurse's office," she said. "Get that looked at, a young man should never have to jerk off with the wrong hand." I thought about my reflection in the glass door outside, and the old man in it looking back at me, and I wondered if she was making fun of me, calling me a young man.

I started to turn away without taking the note she held out to me, but suddenly I stopped and said, "You never answered my question."

"What question?"

"How do you know you're not dreaming?"

"If you can't tell the difference, you better change your medication."

"I'm not on medication."

"Then maybe you should be." I was still holding the kid's pencil in my left hand. I put the pencil in my pocket and felt the piece of glass I had put there ages ago, then took the note from her and, without looking at it, I stuffed it in my pocket next to the pencil and the piece of glass.

She said, "Without dreams you'd never know you'd slept, you'd think you'd been awake all your life, think how exhausting that would feel. Tell the nurse to give you a sleeping pill."

"If I need a sleeping pill that must mean I'm awake."

"Well, if you're not, be sure to wake up before you take the pill."

As I headed toward the door she said, "Just follow the yellow brick road down the hall."

I thought I must've heard her wrong when I stepped outside and didn't see a yellow brick road. But there was a thick, yellow line running down the center of the corridor that I hadn't seen before. I guess she must've been confused, or maybe it was her idea of a joke, calling it a yellow brick road. Probably a joke. She seemed like a jokey sort. I followed the yellow line for a long time, down corridors, up stairways, down stairways, up corridors, I must've walked through the entire building till the yellow line stopped in the building lobby, at the front door where I had entered. I went outside.

It had stopped snowing, the sun was shining, snow was melting all around me. I decided I didn't need to see a nurse, or to change my medication, or to take a sleeping pill. For the first time in a long time, I felt great. Then a piece of my right arm fell off, leaving a short stub descending from the elbow. The piece of arm wriggled off into a snowbank and disappeared. I thought about running after it, then gave up the idea. Even if I caught it,

I wouldn't know how to reattach it. It would be just one more useless thing I'd have to carry around with me.

For a long time I walked between the buildings, crunching snow beneath my feet. I was lightly clothed but I didn't feel cold. It was a lovely day, mounds of snow brilliant in the sunlight, snow lining the walkways and delicately frosting the tree branches. It must've snowed a long time to have piled up that much snow. I didn't think I had been inside that long. Still, now that I think about it, I must've lived a good piece of my life in that building. I guess I was lucky they didn't lock me out to freeze through half a lifetime of snowstorms.

I had to thank the kind man for letting me in just when the door was closing. I wondered where he'd gone. I'd have to give him a big hug if I ran into him again. Then I began wondering if I really wanted to run into him again. The more I thought about it, the more I questioned his motives. Maybe he wasn't that nice after all. I'm sure there was a reason he let me in, an ulterior motive I was unaware of. I'm not sure why I thought that. Maybe I just thought it on general principle, but I couldn't think of anything specific he did or said that should make me think that. In fact, the more I thought about him, the less specific he seemed.

I tried to remember details about him but I began confusing the details with the woman who had sat beside me in front of the fire. I tried to remember what she looked like, too, but I kept confusing her face with the man's. After a while I began wondering if they were one and the same person, the kind man standing beside me transgendered into the woman sitting beside me, and vice versa, back and forth, from one moment to the next. Maybe that's what they weren't telling me. It was all a big practical joke at my expense. Forget the big hug. I'd kick his ass if I came across him, or her ass if it came to that.

The snow was melting fast, the walkways were black and slick with melted ice water, and soon my shoes were soaked through, my feet numb with cold. By now I had recovered all five senses, maybe a couple more than five, and now I could feel the pain. Different sensations had been coming back to me one by one, ever since I had heard the long, low note back at the farm. I almost wished I could return to the time when I only felt thirst and hunger.

The melted ice water turned into a shallow torrent tugging at my ankles. I broke into a run, splashing through the freezing water that was rapidly rising to my knees. All around me the snow had melted into a shallow lake of ice water that stretched between the buildings. Here and there little ice floes bobbed past me, on their way (I guessed) down to the river. Unless the river itself had risen, surfeited with melted ice, and the little ice floes were going nowhere in particular.

I wondered how melted ice water would mix with that strange river water, which I knew was more air than water, maybe even more air than air, so maybe the ice water would sink to the bottom (if there was a bottom) and raise the level of the air water above it. Then the whole NIV would be flooded with air water, and I guessed I could live with that, even hoped it might dry me off. But what if the ice water didn't sink to the bottom (if there was a bottom), but floated on top like the boat I came in on?And the ice water flooding the NIV would continue to rise.

I looked around for higher ground, but it was all pretty flat here. I tried some of the doors, but they were all locked. People peered out the windows of the upper stories, and I shouted up at them to come down and open doors for me. Some of them looked at each other and pointed at me, others shouted back at me, but I couldn't understand what they were saying and none of them backed out of their windows. Pretending not to hear me, I guess. Maybe the ones shouting back at me were crying to me for help but I didn't know what they expected me to do. If I could splash around knee-deep in ice water I guess they could, too.

Then I came to a tall evergreen tree with low branches and hoisted myself up on a branch. It wasn't easy with only one good arm. I had to pull myself up and at the same time jump as high as I could, till I could throw one leg over the branch. It was more a matter of timing than brute strength. As the water rose, I climbed to higher branches. Soon the water must've risen over twenty feet above the ground and I was running out of branches. I reached the last branch and found it was occupied. She was straddling the branch, leaning against the trunk.

"There you are," she said before I could get over my surprise. "I was wondering where you'd gone off to."

"I didn't go off to anywhere," I said. "I stayed in the boat, what happened to you?"

The branch creaked, and I wondered if it would bear the weight of both of us. I clambered down to a lower branch and sat astride it just below her, and leaned against the trunk. Her right foot dangled in front of my face, her sneakers clean and dry, not a speck of mud on them.

"I went on ahead," she said. "I waited for you, but you never showed up."

That wasn't how I remembered it, but I was so used to her lies I didn't care anymore. I thought of all kinds of things I could have said: Did you swim ahead? Did you catch a faster boat? Did you walk along the river bottom faster than I could row? Maybe in an instant you jumped through space and time from one place to another. But I didn't say anything.

I wanted to reach out and fondle her foot but I didn't do that, either, and not just because I needed my one hand to balance myself on the branch. I wouldn't have done it even if I'd had both hands to do it with. I knew by now that, if I wanted something enough, the safest thing was to do nothing.

I craned my head upward to see her face, but it was hidden in the foliage. I had almost forgotten what she looked like. I guess I should've paid closer attention to her.

I said, "It looks like we're stuck together again till the waters recede."

"Oh, they won't do that," she said.

I wasn't sure I heard her right, then after thinking about it a moment, I decided I had. "You mean we're stuck here forever?"

"No, I mean the waters aren't ever going to recede." Then she began chanting quietly and tonelessly: "I never wanted to be a tree, standing there year after year, my roots rotting out from under me..."

"Where did you hear that?" I said.

"It's been going around."

"That's the second time I've heard it today."

"Only the second time? Everybody's singing it."

"You mean there's music that goes with it?"

"They were playing it back at the mall, don't you remember? We danced to it, it's our song."

Now I knew she was lying, and I was about to let go of my branch and grab her foot and pull her off her branch and probably knock us both into the freezing water, when she said, "There it is." I looked down and saw the rowboat nuzzling the boughs of the lower branches.

"How did it know how to get here?" I said.

"It doesn't know anything. It's just a rowboat."

It must've been remote controlled or something, I thought, with all that crazy machinery hidden beneath it, but of course she'd never tell me that. We got down into the boat and she took her place at the oars. I wondered why she pulled so vigorously. She must've known she could work them just by touching an oar with a finger. But I didn't ask. She would've come up with another evasive answer, or not answered at all. Maybe she just liked rowing.

The flood waters had risen to the third or fourth stories of the buildings. People crowded at the windows and waved down at us as we surged past. I wondered if they were just being friendly, or if they were trying to tell us something.

"What's going to happen to them?" I asked, remembering she had said the waters wouldn't recede, but of course I didn't expect an answer and didn't get one. I was left alone with my own speculations. They would wait for rescue boats, rescue wouldn't come, some would try swimming, they would never reach land, they would drown. Some would build rafts from materials they found in the buildings. They would eat up any food they found. They would drink the last of the bottled water, and then they would drink contaminated flood water, or they would build fires to boil the flood water, and burn down the building. When they ran out of food, they would eat each other. The last man standing (of course it would be a man) would commit suicide. He would search for hours till he found a roll of nylon cord in a maintenance closet. The wrapper around the cord said the test strength was five hundred pounds, but he didn't know that meant five hundred pounds dead weight. He shoved a heavy wooden desk under a window, tied one end of the cord to a leg of the desk, tied the other end around his neck and jumped out the window. The instant he reached the end of the cord, his effective weight from acceleration was well over five hundred pounds, or the label lied. The cord snapped, breaking not his neck but his jaw, and still conscious the man died a slow death by drowning, rather than a quick death by hanging.

I tried to think up other scenarios, the more horrible the better, but I guess my imagination was too limited. I'm sure the one I had thought up was from a movie I had seen, or maybe dozens of movies all with the same idea, but I couldn't think of a single title. Maybe they were all too much alike to keep separate. At least I found out this much about myself — I had seen a lot of movies in my life, maybe too many.

But for a moment the scenario had seemed so real, I almost thought I was that last man standing, jumping out the window.

But after the cord snapped, I realized that couldn't be me, since no man can be a witness to his own death after he's died, no matter what they tell you, and a moment later I was back in the rowboat again.

We had left the NIV far behind, and open water stretched forever before us. I craned around and in the distance smoke was rising from black silhouettes of buildings. I thought, It's really happening.

I wondered if this was the same river I had rowed in on. Somewhere I had heard you can't step in the same river twice. I forget where I had heard that one. But I think what I had heard only mentioned stepping in it, because I don't remember hearing anything about rowing on it.

The sun was a little past noon and my little spit of shadow was pointing in the direction we were heading. I wondered if I was finally heading home but I wasn't too hopeful. I didn't remember any large bodies of water near the town and I didn't think I could get there in a rowboat. Unless the town was flooded, too. Maybe the earth really had stopped turning, and the oceans had overwhelmed the continents. But there should have been a mile-high tidal wave, not just ice water trickling out of snow banks.

I dipped my hand into the water. It was cool but not icy. It felt like ordinary water, not the air water we rowed in on. So maybe it was a different river. I scooped up a handful and brought it up to my face.

"Don't drink the water," she said.

"What's wrong with it?"

"You know what's wrong with it."

"No, I don't, and I'm sick of you telling me not to drink it when you won't tell me what's wrong with it."

"Go ahead, drink it, you'll see."

I brought the water to my nose and sniffed at it. It didn't smell like anything in particular, but by now most of it had drained from the cup of my hand. I started to reach down to scoop up another handful, when I noticed little blisters on my palm. I wiped my hand on my pants leg and looked up at her. I expected her face to say I told you so, but her eyes only blinked as she moved backwards and forwards with the motion of the oars.

She was pulling fast, though she hardly seemed to break a sweat, and she never seemed to get tired. I thought maybe the rowing mechanism was broken, which means that, with only one good arm and a blistered hand, I wouldn't be able to take over if she needed a break or decided to disappear again.

The water all around was smooth as glass, but we hardly left a ripple behind us, so maybe we weren't going as fast as her rowing had made me think. The water near us was murky green, but farther out the sun cast a brilliant yellow reflection all around, and the sea (if it was a sea) almost seemed to be burning up. I thought, This is how it's going to end, the sea (if that's what it is) will consume us in its flames.

She kept rowing silently for a while, blinking at me with her great, dark eyes, then she said, "We both want the same thing, you know."

"You mean you want to go home, too?" I said.

"No. Is that what you want?"

"What do you think I've been doing all afternoon?"

"Leaving home."

"Is that what you've been doing?"

She didn't answer. She stopped rowing, and we sat without moving for a while on that glassy plain of burning water. At least I thought we had stopped moving. I could hardly tell the difference between moving and sitting still. Then she began pulling on just one oar. My shadow moved around me past the remnant of my arm and I knew we were turning around, though I still had no sensation of motion. I wondered how she had disengaged the oars so that one oar could move without the other.

"What are you doing?" I said.

"Don't you want to go home?"

"I'm not going back there."

So she kept pulling on her oar till we had made a full circle.

"We can't just keep going round and round, either," I said.

"Why not?"

"We've got to keep moving forward."

"Which way is forward?"

"Any way that doesn't go back. Or around in circles." So she took up both oars again and began rowing more or less in the direction we had been heading, at least according to my shadow.

I was surprised how compliant she had become. I had expected her to ignore my complaints or to reply with one of her cryptic remarks, but now she seemed willing to do whatever I wanted. Maybe she was trying to convince me she had the same goal as I did. Of course I didn't trust her. She was just trying to lull me into another trap. Making me believe she was taking me home, when she had been leading me farther and farther away.

"So where are we going?" I said.

"I'm just going where you're going."

Which didn't make much sense, since she'd done most of the driving so far and kept popping up ahead of me, but I didn't think I'd get anything more out of her. Like the boat going round and round, she could talk in circles as easily as she could row.

Then I heard a scraping sound and looked down in the water. We were skimming inches above a sunken mud bank and sometimes touching bottom. The shoal seemed to go on for miles but she kept rowing as energetically as ever. After a while the mud bank rose to the surface and we ground to a halt. She kept on rowing but the tips of the oars scraped uselessly in the mud.

I said, "We have to go back," but she didn't say anything and kept rowing. I turned around and looked in the direction we had come. Gleaming mudflats stretched in every direction as far as I could see. "The tide must've gone out. We'll have to wait till the tide comes back in." That could be hours, I thought, or given the tardiness of time in these parts, that could be an eternity.

"There's no tides here," she said. She said it in the same sure voice as when she told me back at the mall that it never rained there, or at the NIV that the waters would never recede, and of course I didn't believe her then and didn't believe her now.

I didn't say anything and she kept on rowing, or rather scraping up mud with the oars. And then the boat actually seemed to move slightly. I hardly felt the motion at first, but it was a stronger sensation of motion than when we were crossing the water. I guess the mechanism (whatever it was) hidden beneath the boat was starting to kick in. I wondered what took it so long. Maybe it needed a tune-up.

She seemed unsurprised we were moving and she kept on rowing, jabbing the oars in the mud. Soon we were sledding across the mudflat and splashing through pools of water. It seemed as if we kept on like this for hours, though the sun hadn't moved and my shadow hadn't lengthened. I began thinking about the mall parking lot, the mountain I had climbed, the marsh I had crawled across on that bucking boardwalk, the lake I had waded through, and I knew all these things had an end, sometimes an end coming sooner than I had expected. So now I knew what it meant for time to have an end. Time, like the parking lot at the mall, was just a big expanse of nothing that had to be crossed till it stopped at the edge of some other big expanse of nothing. But these mudflats never seemed to end. They were the largest expanse of nothing I had yet come across. Maybe they were the end that time had to have and it was an end that never ended. But she seemed unconcerned and kept on rowing.

Then we almost bumped into a tree. So I was wrong again. Even unending ends have an end. I hadn't noticed trees on the horizon, but there it was, and then another and another. Maybe they had just sprouted instantly from the mud. All those trees made me think of that dumb song: I never wanted to be a tree, my roots rotting out from under me, or however it went.

Soon they were so thick around us, we couldn't go any farther. They didn't look like any normal trees I had ever seen. They looked artificial and emitted an evil smell and they reminded me of the woods I had met by the marsh. Then I thought maybe these are those woods and the thought terrified me.

"I'm not getting out of this boat," I said. And then a moment later, "We have to get out of here."

But we were hemmed in on all sides. More trees must've sprouted behind us and closed us off from the mudflat. Overhead the canopy shut out most of the sunlight and I no longer had a shadow to guide me. The leaves looked like stylized plastic-coated cardboard cutouts of leaves, and the trunks like molded plastic oozing foul-smelling, oily stuff. She got out of the boat and stood calmly looking at me, her calmness making me ashamed of my cowardice. But she didn't do anything. I guess she was leaving it all up to me now.

"Let's turn the boat over," I said. "Maybe there's something useful underneath."

I wasn't sure if I knew how to make use of anything useful underneath, but in any case I was curious about what kind of engine it had. The last time I tried to turn it over it wouldn't budge, but despite her small size my partner had shown how strong she was, so maybe the two of us could flip it. To my surprise it turned over easily, almost as if it had wanted to, but there was nothing underneath except the bare hull grooved and scratched from sledding across the mud. I rapped on the surface. It sounded hollow.

"It must've fallen off," I said, but I didn't see any marks where an engine might have been attached. I looked around in the gloom but didn't see any machine parts. "How did it run?" I said. "What drove it?" She shrugged as if she had never thought about it.

"How can you not be interested in something like that?" I said. I really wanted to hit her now, not so much from anger at her, but mostly from panic. My last hope had vanished, the hope of a simple mechanical explanation for everything. "Never mind," I said. "I know where we are, I recognize the smell, we're in the woods just across the marsh from your place, we'll find the boardwalk and cross over, I'm taking you back to the farm, and let's hope you stay there, you and those freaks celebrating your fucking moon dog day."

But she was shaking her head. "We can't," she said.

"What do you mean we can't? Did somebody buy the farm?"

"It's gone," she said. "It's not there anymore."

"How can it be gone? Where did it go?"

"It didn't *go* anywhere," she said. "It's just gone."

I must've been like the kid who asks, Where do you go after you die? Uncle, who's an atheist, says, You don't *go* anywhere, it's like the flame of a candle when you snuff it out. The flame doesn't *go* anywhere, it's just *gone*. Then mom comes in and yells at uncle for scaring the kid, though just about nobody is scarier than mom, who tells the kid, Good people fly off with the angels when they die, but you (she says to uncle) — you're going straight to hell. I don't know why I'm remembering all this. If I'm not remembering, then maybe I'm just making it up. But if I am remembering, it must've happened to me, because that's not the kind of thing you see at the movies.

I didn't expect an answer from her but I wouldn't have gotten one from her even if she had wanted to give me one, because just then a loud sneeze came out of the woods, and then another one, and another. All around us, a chorus of sneezes, hundreds, then thousands, a solid wall of deafening sneezes, never ending. We stood there in the darkness holding each other. Or rather I squeezed her in my one good arm while she rested her hands lightly on my back. The sneezing went on for a long time but when nothing happened we gradually loosened our hold on each other, and suddenly the sneezing stopped.

A moment later something coughed in the woods. It was no ordinary cough, but one that reached deep into the lungs (and somewhere there must have been lungs which that cough reached into) and ejected a gigantic, moist, rattling gob of phlegm, and then a thousand other coughs joined in and soon the woods rumbled all around with endless coughing. It was no longer terrifying, it had become just another stupid joke, a lot of phony-baloney make-believe in bad taste, not that I really know what good taste is like.

"You made your point," I yelled into the woods, "Now fucking die already."

And sure enough the coughing stopped. I don't know whether it stopped because I called its bluff (whatever the bluff was), or whether it just got tired of coughing. Or maybe it really did die, it definitely sounded like it was about to. I thought that was something my partner would know, since she seemed to know her way around these parts better than I did. But she had grabbed hold of me again when the coughing started and hadn't let go yet, her face buried in my chest.

Then I thought maybe she knew less than I did but was better at hiding her ignorance. Or maybe she knew only what I knew: she knew I shouldn't drink the water because maybe I already knew I shouldn't, and she knew the flood wouldn't recede because I had already decided it wouldn't, and she kept popping up out of nowhere and disappearing into nowhere whenever I wanted her to, even though I didn't remember knowing, deciding or wanting any of those things, and she still had her face buried in my chest because that's where I wanted her face to be, at least for starters.

Just then something stirred in the canopy, maybe a breeze sprang up or some creature was jumping through the tree tops, or maybe the tree was just trying to shift to a more comfortable position. Whatever, the canopy gaped open to the sky just enough to let a beam of sunlight come down. The beam struck the base of a tree, and the tree began screaming and smoking where the sunlight hit it. A few other screams joined in, but before the whole chorus joined in, the sunlight shifted to the forest floor and the woods fell silent. I suddenly pushed her away from me and dug in my pocket for the piece of glass.

"Cover your ears," I said. When the next sliver of sunlight fluttered towards me, I caught it in the glass and focused the beam back on the tree again. The tree exploded into flames and oily smoke, and the screaming was indescribable, so I won't describe it, unless saying it's indescribable is describing it. The other trees shrunk away from the burning tree, which made the gap in the canopy wider and let more sunlight in and more trees burst into flames. The screaming let up a little, and now I heard a lot of loud sobbing and gasping, but I felt no pity for the stupid things, whatever they were. I grabbed her arm and ran with her through the flames, and suddenly we were out in the open. I stopped and looked back. The burning woods, shrouded in a thick, black column of smoke, were on the other side of a field of cropped grass, a golf course, maybe, and I didn't remember crossing the distance. I guess we were in such a hurry to get away, we didn't notice where we were going.

I had expected we'd be back on the mudflats, which was not a place I wanted to be without the boat. I guess the boat had burned up back there, but I wouldn't have been surprised if it had just flipped right side up again on its own and floated off through the flames. And we definitely weren't on the mudflats now, and those woods were not the ones I had seen near the marsh.

I heard sirens moving toward the column of black smoke. I hadn't heard sirens in centuries, it seemed, and that familiar sound of disaster in the making was somehow reassuring, reminding me of home. We were coming to a suburban neighborhood of tree-lined avenues, sloping lawns and spacious houses with three-car garages. A few people had stepped outside their houses and were looking toward the column of smoke. I almost felt guilty for making them worry — such a quiet, orderly, beautifully manicured neighborhood, all up in smoke if the fire spread. But I didn't feel all that guilty. I was pretty sure if I asked for a glass of water here, they'd take one look at my sunburned face, my singed eyebrows, my sooty, mud-spattered clothing, nearly half an arm missing, the other arm scratched and blistered, and they'd go screaming for the cops, and I'd had about as much screaming as I could put up with in one afternoon. But probably that fire in the distance was the only excitement they'd had around here in a long time, so maybe I had done them a favor burning down their woods.

We started up the street. Some of the people saw us, and when I stared at them, they backed slowly into their houses, but one old man waved us over to the edge of the lawn he was standing on and asked what was going on back there. I told him about the fire without telling him I was the cause of it, and he said, "You look like hell — and you don't even know what hell looks like." Which I thought was a pretty strange thing to say. For a moment I thought he looked like the old man I saw reflected in the glass door back at the NIV, and he might've been talking about himself.

I wondered if I could play on his pity and ask for that glass of water, but before I could speak my partner touched my arm. I looked down at her, she shook her head slightly, and I looked back at the old man. He must've had a serious case of rabbit-eye. His eyes were flaming red, yellow pus oozing out the corners. He saw me and my partner exchanging looks, and he snickered. A boney, clawed hand suddenly snaked out of his coat sleeve and touched the tip of my stump. For the first time I felt pain there, an intense burning sensation that slowly faded after I jerked away from his touch.

"You live by fire, you die by fire," he said, and then in a sudden weepy tone, "Did you have to burn it all down?" I don't know how he knew, but somehow he did, and I didn't try to lie about it.

"It was already sick," I said. "It was an act of mercy."

"How about we show *you* some mercy?"

"I'm not sick."

"How about you get sick?"

We got away from him and hurried on up the street. I looked back and saw he was following us, and some of his neighbors had joined him. More people came out of their houses and stood there watching us. Some of them were holding baseball bats, tennis rackets, hockey sticks, number nine irons — they must've been a real sports-loving bunch of people — and one woman had a pickax hoisted on her shoulder. Trying to be a working-class hero, I guess. I was sure I had seen this movie, too, but I couldn't remember which one it was. Return of the pod people, or some such thing. Are they angry I burned down their woods? How could they all know I was the one who did it? Of course that was a dumb question. Around these parts you couldn't depend on anybody not knowing less about you than you knew about yourself.

The street ended in a cul-de-sac. I turned around and yelled at the people following us. "I'm glad I burned it down, I hope you all burn, too."

I reached in my pocket and pulled out the lump of glass and held it up to the sun. Bright beams of sunlight glanced around the street. Nothing burned, but the people stopped following us. A few of them shrugged and walked back down the street. The old man grinned and wagged his finger at us. The woman suddenly looked embarrassed holding the pickax. A couple of men booed. From one of the houses on the cul-de-sac a man walked down to the street where we stood.

"Don't mind them," he said, smiling. "They hardly ever get a chance to play tough."

I waved the lump of glass at him. Light beams bounced off his face and he winced, but he kept smiling, and then I recognized the kind man from the NIV who had let me in out of the cold. I was abashed at my rudeness and pocketed the glass.

"I thought you'd all been swept away in the flood," I said.

"Not at all," he said. "Except the phrenomenology professor you demolished at the faculty debate. He threw himself off the building with a noose around his neck, the rope broke and he drowned." The portly pipe-smoking man, I thought. Or maybe the portly pipe-stem-crunching man. It had really happened to him, I hadn't imagined it. Or maybe I had imagined it and that's why it happened, but I didn't remember imagining it had happened to him. "The rest of us just waited for the waters to recede," said the kind man.

I looked at my partner. "You said the waters wouldn't recede."

"They didn't recede," she said.

"Let's just say they both did and didn't," said the kind man affably.

"That's not possible," I said.

"Well, if it happened, it has to be possible, doesn't it? Or we have to allow for the inherent ambiguity of the word 'recede', or maybe the word 'water', or both." So I did allow it, remembering how she said it never rained at the mall, when it did. Maybe she had problems with the words recede, rain and water. Watery words. Words that flowed through her brain like airy river water, never meaning the same thing from one moment to the next, like the river that was never the same river each time you stepped in it. I hoped her problems were limited to those words, otherwise we'd have a worse breakdown in communication than we already had.

He invited us into the house, and thinking about that glass of water, I almost accepted, when my partner touched my arm, and this time she didn't even have to shake her head.

"Well, your little friend has other plans," said the kind man when he saw her touching me, and for the first time I thought I heard sarcasm in his voice. The sirens were louder and I looked down the street at the column of black smoke, which had moved closer to the neighborhood. Most the neighbors had drifted back down the street, but not the woman with the pickax, who stood looking at the tool as if she wasn't sure what she was supposed to do with it.

"Maybe we should all just get away from here," I said. "Till the fire burns out."

"You do that," he said. "But I've had my share of disasters this afternoon, and I think I'll just wait this one out here."

I didn't know how he intended to do that if his house burned down, but then he said it wasn't his house, it was his brother-in-law's, and he was going to stay here until the NIV dried out and he could move back to the campus. Which he'd never stepped foot out of in thirty years, I remembered, so he must be way out of his comfort zone, staying at his brother-in-law's. I didn't know what difference it made whose house it was if it burned with him in it, but he seemed to think that it did make a difference, and I doubted I'd get a better answer than that. He showed us through his garden, or his brother-in-law's garden, and let us out the back gate into a street he said would take us out of town. So now I had another reason to be grateful to him, this kind man who kept opening doors for me, but somehow I didn't feel grateful.

"Little friend?" she said. "He called me your little friend?"

"Cut him some slack," I said. "At least he showed us a way out."

"There is no way out."

"You mean, like the flood waters won't recede?" She didn't say anything, and I went on, "You just don't like being called my little friend. That's why you didn't want to go in his house." For the first time she looked mad, and I began to worry she might be right about something. About what, I couldn't tell. It was enough that she knew something I didn't know. "You think I'm too trusting?" I said.

"No, it's because we're running late."

"Late? Late for what? It's only a little past noon." And I noticed the trees lining the street behind the kind man's brother-in-law's garden. They were just like the trees in the burning woods. Well, good, I thought, they'd explode when the first cinders from the burning woods fell on them. Then I realized they were all standing incombustibly in sunlight, so maybe they were a different fire-resistant variety, or maybe they had been treated with some kind of retardant.

They extended all up and down the street in both directions, and I saw no end of them. I suddenly worried they'd try to take revenge on me for what I did to their burning brethren and I definitely didn't want to walk beneath them, but I didn't see any other way to go, except back through the kind man's brother-in-law's garden gate. But when I turned around, I faced a brick wall and no gates anywhere on this side of the street.

"Maybe you're right," I said. "There's no way out. No way in, either."

"Why are you scared of a few trees?" she said. I was about to say I wasn't, when she said, "Wouldn't you rather be a tree, standing there year after year..." She stopped. "They're coming. Looks like we're on time."

I hadn't heard whatever was coming, and I wondered if I was losing my hearing again. But I couldn't be. I heard her well enough, and she had spoken softly. A large van pulled up beside us and the side door opened. A man stepped out and with a glad cry (at least it sounded glad to my uncertain hearing), my partner broke away from me and ran to the man, who caught her in a big hug. I recognized the man as the one who'd tried to bounce me from that party at the mall where I had first met her, and I thought for sure he'd take her away from me, and I was going to lose her again, but he waved me over after they unclenched, and we all climbed into the van. Somehow it didn't occur to me not to. Too tired of walking and rowing, I guess.

It was a lot roomier inside than it looked on the outside. The entire band was there. The three women saxophone players, three children with banjos, two violinists, one bass fiddle player, a jazz drummer with his drum set, a kettle drummer, a conga drummer, one hammered dulcimer player, and the man with the blue guitar. Fourteen musicians with their instruments, plus myself, my dancing partner, and the party bouncer all crowded together in the van, with room to spare. On the inside it looked as big as a bus, but without any passenger seats.

My partner and I sat on the floor facing the rear, and the bouncer slid the side door shut and climbed into the driver's seat and put the van in gear. The band began playing and my partner, sitting cross-legged beside me, swayed gently, her mouth moving, and I bent down close to hear her. She was singing. I could barely hear the words: I never wanted to be a tree...The noise of the band was terrific, not as bad as the screaming trees, but enough for me to want to jump out. Except I didn't really want to be alone again. I guess I must've thought there was safety in numbers. Not that numbers had done all that much for me today.

We seemed to be moving fast now. I craned around to look out the windshield. We'd left the town behind and were careening along a broad, elevated highway. I wondered if it was the causeway I had walked under earlier this afternoon (if it was still the same afternoon), and for the first time in a long time I almost began to believe I was heading home.

"Where are we going?" I yelled to the driver, but he didn't hear me over the noise. I thumped him on the shoulder and he turned his head and looked at me. The van began zigzagging down the highway but he seemed unconcerned and kept on looking at me. "Keep your eyes on the road," I yelled.

But he didn't hear me. His mouth said, "What?"

I stabbed a finger at the windshield and attempted a steering gesture, but a steering gesture with only one hand and the stub of a forearm probably didn't make much sense, and his mouth said "what?" again, and just then we went off the pavement. The van bounced along a rugged median strip, and for a moment I thought we'd flip over for sure, but he brought us back onto the highway, and the band played on, so I stopped trying to find out from him where we were going. But now he seemed more interested in looking back at me than in keeping his eyes on the road, and the van kept swerving from shoulder to shoulder. Traffic was light, but we were going faster than anyone else, and we barely missed a couple of other vehicles. I think he was waiting for me to reply to his question but of course I couldn't over the din, and he was starting to look annoyed. My frantic gestures at the highway ahead of us only seemed to increase his irritation.

I turned back and yelled at the band to stop playing, but they didn't hear me, either. I crawled over to the kids with banjos and grabbed their instruments out of their hands, then tipped over the hammered dulcimer, the conga drum, the kettle drum, grabbing all the instruments I could except the bass player's, who had been playing almost lying down and had fallen asleep with his arms wrapped around the neck of his instrument. And the jazz drummer's, who whacked me with a mallet when I tried to tip over his high hat. But soon it was silent inside the van, except for my partner singing: "My roots rotting out from under me..."

I turned to the driver and said, "Keep your eyes on the road."

"Why didn't you just say so," he said, turning back to face the windshield. I started to ask him where we were going, when the jazz drummer began working the pedal of the bass drum, and the rest of the band, after retrieving their instruments, started up again.

After that I kept my mouth shut and put up with the noise and waited to see where we were going, which seemed to be nowhere, since the highway went on for miles above a featureless landscape, another vast expanse of nothing. But then a police car pulled in front of us, its siren wailing over the noise of the band, and the cop stuck his arm out, signaling us to stop. At first I thought the siren sound was coming from the band but I couldn't see which instrument was making the noise, and then I looked out the window.

Our driver veered into the next lane and tried to pull ahead of the cop, but the cop spurted ahead and got in front of the van again, and then two other patrol cars pulled up on each side of us. I yelled at our driver to slow down, but of course he didn't hear me this time any better than he did before, and he accelerated until he almost tapped the rear bumper of the cruiser ahead of us. I shook my partner, who was still mouthing the words of the song. I bent close to her ear and shouted, "Get him to stop, he's going to get us all killed." She stopped singing and looked up at me with great, dark, unblinking eyes and said something, not the words of the song, I was sure, but something that was supposed to be reassuring, whatever it was. And suddenly the van slowed. I guess whatever she'd said must've been the right words, and whatever makes things happen here must have heard them, since I'm pretty sure the driver didn't. The driver slammed on the brakes, all the musicians pitched forward almost on top of me, and outside a half dozen cops jumped out of their vehicles and surrounded us, pointing sidearms and shotguns and yelling get out of the fucking car.

I wondered if they knew it was a van, not a car, and that inside it was practically a bus. But maybe car was the right word to use when you were in a hurry, and you had to be brief and use the shortest syllables you could come up with. But that didn't explain why they said car instead of van or bus, which all took pretty much the same amount of time to say, and why did they waste time on the word fucking, which seemed completely beside the point? I guess they wanted to show us how mad they were, and from my own experience I knew getting mad could sometimes speed things up, but often with unpredictable results.

The musicians clambered out of the van looking bewildered, most without their instruments, except the man with the blue guitar, who began playing a melancholy tune on it, the first real music I had heard coming from anyone in the band. But then a cop strolled over and knocked him down and grabbed his guitar and smashed it against the side of the van. Bits of blue guitar hit the cop in the face, and he turned and grinned at me and said, "Now, that's assault with a deadly weapon." I didn't know if he was calling himself an assailant and the guitar a deadly weapon, or the guitar was the assailant and its music a deadly weapon. But I didn't think the guitarist's music was all that bad. It was even somewhat soothing. Maybe the shattered pieces of the blue guitar were deadly weapons, but he'd said *a* deadly weapon, not several deadly weapons, and the pieces that had hit him hardly raised a welt on his face. But maybe the cop had heard the band playing when he was chasing us, and I guess that could sound pretty deadly, even from a distance. But mostly the cops ignored the musicians, who just stood around looking awkward and abashed.

The cops seemed more interested in me. They half surrounded me, their hands on their hips, then the grinning cop dragged me up to his vehicle and slammed me against the side and said, "Put your hands on the car."

I put a hand on the car and he said, "Both hands."

"The other hand is missing," I said.

He grinned and said, "Driving with only one hand? That's a violation."

"I wasn't driving."

He began patting me down. He pulled the lump of glass out of my pocket, looked at it curiously for a moment and said, "What's this? Concealed weapon?"

"Accelerant," said another cop. "Looks like we caught ourselves a firebug."

"Nah, looks like an arsonist to me," said the grinning cop and pocketed the evidence. He took out the pencil I had snatched from the kid back at the NIV. "Now this — that's a concealed weapon." And then the note the woman in the bright, blue pants suit had written for me. He looked at it a long time and then pocketed it: "Passing off phony scrip — you dealing, punk?"

"Why are you doing this? I haven't done anything."

"Along with everything else you haven't done? The way you were driving, speeding, reckless endangerment, attempted vehicular manslaughter..."

"But I wasn't driving."

"A dozen witnesses say you were." I looked over at the musicians, silent, shuffling, crestfallen, their hands twitching for their instruments.

"They haven't said anything," I said.

"They will."

I looked around for the driver but didn't see him anywhere. Or my partner, either. I guess she'd pulled another disappearing act and taken him along with her. Or maybe he'd taken her along with him. I should've known they were in it together, the way they got into that clench after he'd pulled up in the van. Why was I not surprised? Just when I was beginning to hope I'd see home again.

I looked at the cop and realized how much he looked like the driver, maybe he was the driver, and the unfairness of it all suddenly overwhelmed me, and all I could think of was to say, "But how do *you* know you're not dreaming?"

He kept grinning when he said, "Because I never dream about assholes like you, sweetheart."

He shoved me into the back of the car and we took off, the other cop cars following. I looked out the back window and saw the musicians standing next to the van, abandoned in the middle of the highway, cars and trucks zooming past them on both sides, horns blaring. The musicians drove me crazy when I was with them in the van, but now I began to worry about them, they seemed so helpless. I wondered if anyone among them knew how to drive.

The police cruiser must've gone a lot faster than I had realized, because before I knew it we were off the highway and pulling up in front of a grimy, yellow, two-story building. Maybe I just had a memory lapse, one of those moments when, or maybe where, you take your time getting somewhere, but when you look back it seems like no time at all. Or maybe time really can fold in on itself, and great distances are covered in an instant. But I was getting used to the experience, even hoping it would happen more often and get me home sooner.

The grinning cop got out and came around, and as he pulled me out of the car, I looked up at the sky where the sun still stood at a little past noon. He bent my arm behind my back and handcuffed it but couldn't find another wrist to cuff it to, so he just let the cuffs dangle off my wrist and pushed me into the building, down a gloomy, green corridor that smelled of floor polish, and into a gloomy, gray room that smelled of disinfectant. In the ceiling, a single incandescent bulb enclosed in steel mesh dimly lit the room. He propelled me behind a metal table bolted to the floor and shoved me into a metal chair also bolted to the floor and cuffed me to a small, steel horseshoe bolted upright to the table top, then grinned at me one last time and walked out, slamming the door.

It was moments like that when I wished the memory lapse or time lapse (whatever it was) would happen, because I sat there a long time, and nothing happened. This entire afternoon, however many centuries it had lasted, something was always happening, even if it was only me walking or crawling or rowing around on those wide expanses of nothing. But this time nothing happened. Maybe that wide expanse of nothing I was crawling around on was nothing but the nothing that was happening now, without my crawling around on it.

I shouted to the empty room, "Could I have some water please?" But of course nobody came. Suddenly I needed to pee and wondered, Why now? When I'd had an eternity and an endless wilderness to pee in. With one hand chained to the table top and the other hand missing, I couldn't even open my fly to pee on the floor, which would have served them right (whoever they were). But I guess this was just some new torture they (whatever they were) had dreamed up. Dreamed was the right word here. How could I know I wasn't dreaming? By the continuity of things, which only dreams can interrupt. And since nothing this afternoon had much continuity, the whole thing must've been a dream. Those time and memory lapses were a giveaway.

But what about the times between the lapses? There was plenty of continuity there, one thing happening after another according to whatever bizarre laws of physics governed them. But that was another giveaway. What laws of physics, however strange, would keep the sun riveted to one place in the sky while you row across a mudflat with self-propelling oars? Only a dream could come up with a dumb idea like that.

These thoughts comforted me as I sat there chained to the table top, wanting to pee, and almost believing I would soon wake

up. Maybe wake up in my own bed, unglue my eyelids, look up
at the ceiling, stretch, yawn. Stagger into the bathroom and void
the flood dammed up in me. I tried to remember what my bed
was like, the color of the sheets, the texture of the fabric, the
lumps in the mattress, the sour fragrance of the pillows. I closed
my eyes and tried to imagine the bedroom, but I only got a vague
image of the room I was sitting in now, though without the
handcuffs and the bolted-down table and chair. And I opened my
eyes and looked at my chained-down arm, its blisters and welts,
and I thought: I got those a long time ago, before my last memory
lapse or time lapse, or whatever it was, and how's that for
continuity? And suddenly I peed in my pants. How's that for
physics?

The door opened and a man in plain clothes walked in.
Halfway across the room he paused, sniffed the air, wrinkled his
nose and shook his head.

"The board of health ought to shut you down," he said. In his
hand he carried a thick file folder and slapped it down on the
table. "But at least we finally caught up with the one-armed man."

I recognized my dancing partner's old boyfriend from the
farmhouse. She had said the farmhouse no longer existed, at least
I think that's what she had said, but, whatever, I was sorry to see
some of its former tenants were still around.

"I should've known you were a cop," I said.

"Should've, could've, would've, but didn't, go figure" he said
sitting down opposite me and opening the file folder. "With a
record that could fill a phone book." He started turning the pages
of a magazine inside the file folder.

I said, "I've never had a problem with the police before."

"How can you be so sure?" He looked up from the magazine.
"Since you don't even know whether you're dreaming or not."

"I never said I didn't know, I was just asking others how they
know."

He looked back down at the magazine and began slowly turning the pages, pausing briefly every now and then to smile or frown or shake his head at something he saw.

Without looking up he said, "Why do you go around asking, if you're already so sure?"

I saw handwriting in the margins and in the white spaces of the magazine and realized he was looking at the essay I had written back at the NIV. From under the magazine he pulled out three small plastic bags. They contained the lump of glass, the pencil, and the note the grinning cop had taken from me. He held up the lump of glass and smiled, then the note and frowned, then the pencil and shook his head.

"The pen is mightier than the sword," he said, "but only if we can read your handwriting."

"That's a pencil, not a pen."

"Which you failed to return to its rightful owner. You know that kid is still looking for his pencil? How does that make you feel?"

"Awful."

"Awful? That's the best you can come up with? Awful. Have you no shame?"

"Just read me my rights and get me a lawyer, or let me go," I said.

He closed the folder and stood up, clenching the folder in both hands.

"Let you what?" he said and whacked me across the head with the folder. It almost felt more like an electric shock than a blow with a soft object. "Get you a what?" Whack again. "How about I read you this?" One last whack, and he turned around and walked out.

The whacks were more surprising than painful, but most surprising of all was how I could feel them after a long afternoon of feeling almost nothing, and that worried me — more evidence

I wasn't dreaming, or if I was I wouldn't be waking up any time soon, since three stiff whacks across the head should wake anybody up, even if I was only dreaming them. After that I spent a long time, hours, days, years, sitting there trying to figure out how sure I really was that I wasn't dreaming, shivering in my peed-in pants, and when I saw the faint wisps of my own breath, I realized it was getting colder in the room.

Then the boyfriend came back in. He carried the same file folder, somewhat thicker now than before, and what looked like the charred remnants of an oar.

"Remember this?" he said, thumping the table with the oar. It was a three-foot piece of the paddle end, but inside its coat of black char it seemed sturdy enough, judging from the sound it made on the table. "I know you do," he said, setting the oar on the table between us. "And I know you know what it can do." I wondered if he meant it could do a better job of whacking than the file folder. He sat down in front of me.

"Row," I said. He looked at me incredulously. "It can row, I mean it could row, it doesn't look like it can do much of anything now."

"Don't be so sure," he said.

"It definitely looks like it's had better days."

"That we can both agree on, and that's why we're adding the charge of theft."

"I didn't steal it, your girlfriend said she got it upriver just around the bend."

"My what?" He looked like he was about to stand up again, then relaxed, silently fingering the oar in front of him. I guess he was deciding to prolong the mental torture before he started on the physical stuff again. Then he opened the file folder and took out the magazine, the one I had written in at the NIV, and for the first time I saw in it the article entitled "How Do You Know You're Not Dreaming?", which I had never had a chance to finish. I wondered why I hadn't noticed it when I had written in the magazine back then. Maybe that was before I'd learned how to read. I leaned forward trying to read the answer to the title question, but he shoved the magazine beneath the open cover of the file folder and took out a sheet of paper and slid it toward me.

"Is that your signature?" I recognized the document the little man from the delivery service tried to get me to sign when he delivered the hatbox (if that's what it was).

"It says REFUSED on it," I said.

"Is your name REFUSED?"

"No, of course not — ."

"So you accepted the package under false pretenses."

"No, it was addressed to OCCUPANT — "

"Is your name OCCUPANT?"

I didn't say anything, and he said, "So we're adding a charge of — hell, I don't know. Whatever applies." He shoved another piece of paper at me. It said EAT ME in large black letters that covered the entire page. "Did you eat this document?" he said.

"It doesn't look eaten to me."

"Forensics is good at reconstructing evidence, so did you eat this document, yes or no?"

"I don't know, I guess so, or something like it, what difference does it make?"

"Eating it, that's destruction of official government paper, not eating it is a refusal to obey a lawful order."

"What's so lawful about a stupid piece of paper? it's just somebody's idea of a bad joke."

He grabbed the oar and smashed it on the table an inch from my manacled hand.

"The law is no joke," he shouted. Then in a gentler voice he added, "If you thought it was a joke, why did you eat it?"

"I don't know, I guess I was hungry."

"I get it, you have such bad taste in food, you ate the document because you thought it was a joke in bad taste." He seemed to think that was funny, or at least worth a chuckle.

"It said EAT ME, so I took it in good faith and ate it, I'm sorry, I didn't mean to."

"You didn't mean to? What would become of the world if everyone was like you?"

"If everyone was like me — it would be a world without crime, and you would be out of a job."

"That's not going to happen, is it? Since you admit you ate these words, which means you meant to."

"Well, if I ate them I'm in compliance, and if I didn't eat them then I'm also in compliance, either way I'm in compliance." Even as I said it, the argument sounded pretty lame. The detective just shook his head and smiled and didn't say anything. He looked down at the file folder, then at the magazine I had written my essay in, and tapped it gently with a forefinger.

"It doesn't really matter," he said, "we have everything we need right here." He slipped "How Do You Know You're Not Dreaming" back in the folder and closed the cover and picked up the paddle. He looked at the paddle thoughtfully for a moment, tapping it on the table, and then set it down in front of me, just beyond reach of my manacled hand.

"What do you mean, you have everything you need?" I said.

"Your confession."

"I haven't confessed anything."

"It's all in here." He patted the folder in front of him. "In your own handwriting."

"That's not what that says, that's just my answer to an exam question."

"So then you admit to writing it?"

"I'm saying it's not a confession."

"So what does it say?"

That stumped me. I couldn't remember a thing I had said in the essay, if I had said anything at all.

"It's just an exam question."

"So what was the question?"

I couldn't remember what the question was, I couldn't even remember if there was a question, I could only remember the woman in the bright, blue pants suit commenting how nicely illustrated my essay was.

The boyfriend opened the file folder again and said, "This was the question: are you guilty of the crimes herein described? Give details. Describe time, place, manner, motivation and all persons involved, including accomplices and victims." He looked up. "You were very precise with the details."

"You're making it up, that's not what it says."

"Then what does it say?"

"I don't know what it says, but I didn't do those crimes."

"What crimes?"

"The ones there — what you said it says — 'herein described'."

"What crimes are those?"

"How should I know? I haven't even had a chance to read it."

"If you wrote it you must've read it." I didn't say anything. After a moment he took a slip of paper from his jacket pocket. "Don't ask me why, but I'm supposed to read you your rights." He read: "You have the right to remain silent so long as we do not want to hear what you have to say. Anything you say may be held against you in a court of law whether you say it or not. You have the right to an attorney if you can afford one. If you cannot afford an attorney, one will be provided for you who is unable or unwilling to defend your rights..." He went on like this for a long time, much longer than I expected the rights-reading ritual should take, and I lost track of what he was saying. I guess I decided it didn't make any difference whether I kept track or not. He concluded, "Do you understand these rights?"

"No," I said, "I don't understand any of this," and he began reading them all over again. When he asked me again if I understood them, I said, "As well as I did last time."

"I'll take that as a yes," he said and slipped the piece of paper back in his jacket pocket and pocketed the pencil, the piece of glass, and the note the woman in the bright, blue pants suit had written for me. He stood up, gathering the file folder and its contents, and pointed at the paddle in front of me. "I'm leaving this here to remind you this is what your miserable life has finally come to." He headed toward the door.

"I haven't done anything," I yelled.

He stopped at the door and half turned, a puzzled look on his face. "How can anybody not do anything? Even doing nothing is doing something."

Later, hours, days, centuries later, a young woman came in. She walked briskly across the room, puffy blonde hair bouncing against her shoulders. She wore a tweedy brown jacket and carried a large beige purse. She sat down in front of me and set the purse on the floor beside the chair, and reached down in the purse for a fountain pen and notebook.

"I've seen you before," I said. "I just don't remember where."

She looked sharply at me, then uncapped the pen and flipped open the notebook and began writing.

"What are you writing?" I said.

"Making a note how you came on to me as I entered the room."

"How could I come on to you, one hand chained down, the other gone missing, I can't even come on to myself."

She wrote something else down.

"Now what?" I said.

"You rank high in the self-pity category, don't you?"

"Who are you, anyway?"

"I'm your court-appointed psychologist, I'm here to determine if you're competent to stand trial."

"Trial for what? I've never done anything wrong."

She wrote something else down. She wrote in large letters that I could see across the table, "delusional — paranoid", followed by a row of question marks that spread all the way to the edge of the page.

"I'm delusional and paranoid? Just because I never thought I'd be tried for crimes I never committed?"

"Do *you* think you're delusional and paranoid?"

"Isn't it your job to find out?"

She put the pen down and looked at me thoughtfully for a moment. "If you were delusional only at the times you did *not* commit those crimes, then you would be fit to stand trial. You would be found unfit only if you were delusional at the time you *did* commit those crimes. In either case, we need to know right now if you presently have the intellectual capacity to understand the charges being brought against you."

"I'm pretty sure I don't."

"If you're pretty sure, then it's evident that you do understand, because if you didn't understand, then how could you be pretty sure?"

"I mean, the charges have never been read to me, so how can I understand them?"

"That's something you'll have to take up with your lawyer."

"So just one question — how do you know you're not dreaming?"

"How do *I* know? This isn't about me." She picked up the pen again and wrote "hostile attitude", followed by three exclamation marks.

"How does anybody?"

"This isn't about anybody. You're the one facing trial." She wrote "deflecting", and another three exclamation marks.

"I think I rank better than three exclamation marks," I said, and she wrote down "delusions of grandeur", followed by a row of question marks. I guess the question marks meant she was keeping an open mind about it. She capped her pen, closed the notebook, put them back in her purse and stood up.

"That's it?" I said. "So am I fit to stand trial?"

For the first time she showed anger. "I have thousands of subjects to interview, I don't have time for this." She walked briskly from the room, puffy blond hair bouncing against the back of her neck. A little later she came back in. Her eyes were red, as if with weeping. She sat down across from me and pulled out a tissue from her purse and blew her nose.

"I owe you an apology," she said. "I haven't been doing my job, I haven't been doing you justice." She buried her face in her hands and shook her head, as well as anybody could with her face buried like that. Then she raised her head and said, "I know it hasn't been easy for you, and I want to help you, but you have to help me help you."

"Just tell me what I'm supposed to confess, and I'll confess, does that help?"

"We don't do it that way," she said. "Our job is to find the truth, no matter how much it hurts."

"If my job isn't to confess, then how can I help?"

"It's more than confession, it's...it's..." She pulled out another tissue and wiped her eyes. "I asked to be taken off this case, but they sent me right back in here, they told me to keep at it until you — until you — ." She said something else, but I couldn't make out the words through sounds that might have been sobs, or maybe she was just trying to keep from throwing up. She jumped out of her chair and rushed from the room. She had left her purse on the floor beside the chair, and I thought she would come back in and get it, but she never did.

"Until I what?" I said to the empty room.

# WOES MAY DASH WITHIN YEARS

I stood up still chained to the horseshoe and, bending over the table, slid around to the other side. I sat down in her chair and picked her purse up between my feet and lifted it to the table top and nudged it and the paddle against the horseshoe. On this side of the table, my arm was stretched too tight to let my hand do any work, so I slid back around to the other side and sat down in the bolted-down steel chair.

I expected the cops to come charging in at any moment, but they never did. I didn't see any one-way windows in the room, or cameras, or peepholes, or maybe I had been there so long they had forgotten about me, or maybe they were just too bored to watch me.

With my manacled hand I tipped over the purse and scattered the contents in front of me. The notebook, the pen, the pack of tissues, a wallet, a coin purse, a compact, a comb, a tampon, a folded-up newspaper clipping with the headline WOES MAY DASH WITHIN YEARS — I tried to read the story, but the letters kept jumping around too much. The headline didn't make much sense, so I guess the news story wouldn't have, either. I guess my reading skills hadn't improved much since the NIV, though I had been able to read the notes my court-appointed psychologist was making. Just another meaningless trick of the day, I guess.

I hardly expected to find anything useful from her purse, much less a key to unlock the cuffs, but then I found a pair of plyers. I wondered what a court-appointed psychologist was doing with a pair of plyers in her purse. Not that there's anything wrong with that. Plyers are a very useful tool.

With the pliers I tried working the bolts that held down the inverted horseshoe I was chained to, but the bolts were too tight and the plyers kept slipping. I tried biting through the chain with the teeth of the plyers but that hardly scratched the steel. Then using a plyer handle I tried to pry open the bracelet attached to the horseshoe, and the handle broke. I dashed the broken plyers against the table top and they bounced out of reach. I wondered why whoever (whatever they were) even bothered to leave behind a pair of useless plyers for me to find.

Then I started throwing other contents of the purse across the room till I got to the notebook and stopped throwing things, surprised at my own fury, which for some reason seemed undreamlike for a dream. So maybe it wasn't a dream. That much rage in a dream should've awakened any dreamer.

I opened the notebook and found every page blank, nothing in it about self-pity, paranoid delusions, deflecting, or hostile attitudes. She could've swapped out the old notebook for a fresh one when she left the room, but this one seemed exactly like the same notebook, with the same nicks, scratches and doodles on the cover. So maybe it was a dream. I uncapped the pen and added a few doodles of my own and waited for the ink to disappear, but it continued to look like normal, blue, unfading, fountain-pen ink. Just then the door opened and the little man from the delivery service walked in. He stopped and looked around.

"What a dump," he said. Then he looked at me. "What movie is that from?"

"What are you doing here?"

The little man hoisted himself into the interrogator's chair and stood up. "I have an order to recall a package misdelivered to your address," he said.

"Why didn't you take it back when I told you it was misdelivered?"

"I hadn't received the order yet."

"Well, I don't have it with me, I left it at home."

"I know that, so you'll have to go home and get it." He climbed up on the table and crawled across to the horseshoe. He took the chain in two small stubby hands and bit down on it. With a sound like dry noodles breaking, the chain parted in his mouth. Then he grabbed my arm and gnawed on the handcuff bracelet, which broke loose from my wrist and clattered to the table. He sat back and spit out bits of metal. "You need to bring it back by closing time tonight," he said.

"I'm not coming back here."

"What better place than the cop shop? You don't get it back on time, I'll bite your arm off."

I didn't know which arm he meant. I hoped he meant my right arm, what was left of it, which wouldn't have been any great loss. Or maybe he was just kidding, his way of bragging about the strength of his teeth and jaws. He laughed and jumped off the table and waddled quickly out the room. I don't know what the laugh meant. Maybe he didn't believe me, maybe it was a disgusted laugh, maybe a laugh of pity.

I took the woman's notebook and fountain pen and stuffed them in my pocket and grabbed the paddle and trailed after him, but I didn't see him in the gloomy, green corridor. The cold and the hours, years or centuries of inactivity had weakened me so much I kept falling to my knees and had to keep propping myself up with the paddle. The corridor was deserted. I passed empty rooms, dust everywhere, floors littered, chairs overturned, I met no one, the building seemed abandoned. I was afraid I had got lost in another labyrinth but I soon found the front entrance.

The parking lot outside was empty, no cop cars anywhere. I wobbled across the parking lot and out to the street in front. It looked like the street where I had lost my way before I got to the mall. Overhead clouds scudded across the sky. I passed a news rack spray-painted in gray that hadn't been smashed open yet, and I smashed it open with the paddle and pulled out a newspaper headlined ION EYE MASS HARD WITH YAWS. I tried to read the story but the letters kept jumping around, and soon the letters formed a new headline, ONE RASH WAD WAY IS SHY TIME. I slipped the paper back in the rack and wobbled on up the street, or down the street, whichever way it was.

I was slowly regaining strength and started to walk faster, hoping once again I'd be home soon. I came to the restaurant I had passed before, the same people in it having lunch. I wondered if it was the same lunch as the one they were eating last time I saw them. Or maybe they were the same clientele who came here every afternoon for lunch, and many lunches had passed since the first lunch I had seen them eating.

The same bald man sitting near the window was reading a newspaper. This time he was holding it up in the air, facing the window, and I could've read the headline easily if I had tried, but instead I raised the paddle and hit the window as hard as I could. I'm not sure why I did that. Maybe because they hadn't let me in the last time I came by. Maybe because I was sick of reading those stupid headlines.

Jagged cracks like lightning bolts fluttered across the glass, and suddenly the window shattered, thousands of starbursts falling to the sidewalk, glittering in the fitful sunlight. I jumped back into the street as the window frame crumpled and the walls around it began to collapse, dragging the roof down with them. The patrons didn't seem to be paying much attention and kept on eating lunch until they disappeared under a pile of rubble. The buildings on each side of the restaurant began to sag sideways and then fell onto the rubble, and soon all up and down the street the buildings were collapsing, raising a great cloud of dust.

I heard sirens in the distance and guessed the cops were still around and coming closer, and I ran through the cloud of dust, choking and spitting. I came out of the cloud in the middle of a park. I didn't remember a park the last time I came by here, but maybe I took a different turn while running through the cloud. I didn't hear sirens any more. I looked back and didn't see the dust cloud, either. Just trees all around, and some neatly tended hedges.

I hoped I didn't run into any trees like the ones in the burning woods, or the village of the pod people, or whatever they were. But they all looked like ordinary trees, not that I know all that much about trees. But at least I could tell a pine tree from an oak, and the park seemed to have plenty of those, plus a few others that looked familiar but whose names I didn't know. In the distance I heard a noise and followed it for a while, and coming around a clump of rhododendrons (I recognized rhododendrons, too), I saw a large band shell at the end of a clearing. A crowd stood around swaying like tall grass in a breeze. Or maybe the fitful afternoon light was just playing tricks on my eyes.

Everyone from the strip mall was there, all the party guests from the farm, and just about everyone else I had met between here and there. All my friends from the band were up on the stage, playing their hearts out as usual. I was actually happy to see them, since I last saw them in the middle of the freeway, trapped between streams of speeding cars. As long as I stood off at a distance I could even put up with their music.

Then I noticed the man with the blue guitar wasn't there. I hoped he hadn't been injured when the cop knocked him down. Or maybe he was just heartbroken over the loss of his guitar, or maybe he couldn't stand touching someone else's instrument, since nothing on earth can make us happier than playing the instrument we were meant to play. I don't know how I knew that. Maybe I had once played an instrument.

"They're playing our song," she said.

I turned and looked at my dancing partner standing beside me. I wasn't surprised to see her, since by now I was used to her suddenly popping up out of nowhere.

"It isn't *my* song, I can tell you that," I said.

"Did you pee in your pants?"

I was about to hit her with the burnt paddle but she didn't say anything, just looked at me with her great, serious eyes, and I couldn't tell whether that was supposed to be a reproachful gaze, or just a thoughtful one, or maybe a completely empty one.

"What happened to the man with the blue guitar?" I said.

"Who?"

"The man with the blue guitar. I actually liked how he played, at least when I could hear it."

"There's no man with a blue guitar."

"I know that. So what happened to him?"

"How can anything happen to no one?"

I was pretty sure she knew. If I knew what I was talking about, so did she. But I thought it would be pointless pressing her for an answer. We stood silently watching the band for a while, and then I said, "Do they ever play anything else?"

"Why should they?" She said. She seemed about to say something else, but then she said, "Oh, I'm on!" and dashed toward the stage. She climbed up and faced the crowd and stood with her back to the bass player, who moved his fingers about once every ten seconds or so, always plucking the same string. She began singing. The band drowned out her voice but, as I moved closer, I saw her lips forming the words to "Our Song", or whatever the name was. By now I had heard it so many times I never failed to recognize it even when I couldn't hear it.

"So how do *you* know you're not dreaming?" said someone standing behind me. I turned and looked at the boyfriend. I wondered if he was going to take me back into custody, and I raised the burnt paddle, ready to whack his head off if he made any moves. But he just stood there smirking, his hands in his pocket. "You keep asking everybody, but you never ask how *you* know. So I'm guessing that's not what you really want to know."

"So what is it I really want to know, according to you?"

"Just take a pill."

I whacked him as hard as I could. I hoped he wasn't still a cop. Not that it would matter if they got me for assaulting a police officer, on top of everything else. But you never knew what anybody really was around here, where everyone but me could pick and choose whatever parts they wanted to play. Or maybe this world was just a shoestring theater where actors had to double up on the roles.

"Take the whole bottle," he said. It was as if I had hit him with a straw. He barely blinked. Actually he did blink once, but slowly, unsurprised, so I hit him again, and his smirk grew into a grin.

"Violence won't get you anywhere," he said.

"Nothing else does, either," I said and I hit him again, thinking third time is a charm, but it wasn't. Neither was the fourth time, or the fifth.

"But then again, pain teaches us about the world," he said. "Fortunately, pleasure helps us put up with it."

"Which one is this?" I said and hit him again. He wiped his face, so maybe I was finally getting to him, though I would've preferred he just fell down and died.

"You've got a lot of anger in you," he said.

"Where else should it be?"

"You start out looting news racks and end up wrecking a whole town, but you've got to realize you can't really do that."

I was about to tell him that I could and deny that I had. But a moment later I was standing in front of that same restaurant, looking in at the same people eating lunch. At least I think it was the same restaurant and the same people. But the back wall of the restaurant looked somewhat like the band shell, and the people were not eating lunch. They were all standing facing the back, or facing the band shell, or whatever it was they were facing. It was all probably just a trick of the light reflected on the window glass. I guess the boyfriend was trying to prove I hadn't really wrecked the whole town. Or maybe I was being given another chance to do everything all over again, whether I wanted to or not, and whoever was running this show couldn't quite get the scenery right, as usual.

But I didn't want to do any of it all over again. The boyfriend was wrong. I didn't want to take a pill. I didn't want to take the whole bottle. I didn't want to know how I knew I wasn't dreaming. I didn't want to know how I knew I was. I just wanted to get home.

I looked at the paddle I was still holding in my one good hand. I guess I was expected to do something with it, maybe try something spectacular with it and fail, and prove the boyfriend right. So I tossed it into the street. You can't fail if you don't try, you can't lose if you're not in the game, you can't get booed off the stage if you don't play the scene. I don't know where I learned all these pithy phrases, but at least one of them must be true, otherwise why did I take the trouble to learn them?

The paddle struck the pavement and broke into chunks of burnt wood and charcoal. Just then a truck rolled over it and halted a few feet ahead, leaving behind a black smear on the pavement. The little man from the delivery service hopped out.

"Too bad I won't have to bite your arm off," he said.

He went around to the rear of the truck and pulled out a package. He dropped it at my feet and headed back to the front of the truck. The package was addressed to OCCUPANT and marked REFUSED.

"How did you get this?" I said. "How did you get into my apartment?"

"I drove in, how do you think?"

"You admitted it was misdelivered. Why am I getting it back?"

"It wasn't misdelivered. It just had the wrong address on it."

"So maybe you can tell me where the right address is?"

"I only deliver packages, not people"

I was about to tell him I didn't want to be delivered, I only wanted to be pointed in the right direction. But he jumped into the truck and drove off. I stared down at the hatbox (if that's what it was), not willing to risk my one remaining hand trying to undo it. But it looked like it was already half undone. The white tissue paper was torn, the red bowknot had fallen off, and the string was broken. I nudged the package with my toe, and the wrapping suddenly fell off, like dried petals falling off a flower.

Inside was a plain brown cardboard box. I wondered how such a flimsy container could carry something as heavy as it had felt when I had first hefted it. But I nudged it again and it seemed light enough to contain nothing heavier than the hat it was meant to contain. In fact, a sudden gust of wind started shoving it down the street. I hurried after it and grabbed it before it could fly away. I thought I had chased it some distance but when I straightened up, clutching the box, I saw I was still in front of the restaurant. Or maybe it was some other restaurant that looked like the first restaurant. But the more I looked at the restaurant the more it looked like the band shell. My dancing partner was still up there belting out the last inaudible lines of her song.

"You're up next," said the boyfriend beside me.

"I'm not going up there," I said.

The boyfriend looked at the box I was holding. "What, are you going to hit me with that too?"

"Sure," I said, and smashed it into his face.

I guess it was heavier than it felt, since he backed away holding his nose. The lid popped off the box and a head poked out. I dropped the box and the angry ghost I had met back at the farm crawled out. I wondered how such a small box could hold such a big girl, but I guess if you're a ghost, you could fill any space, or no space at all.

"What did you do with it?" she yelled, and if I had kept that paddle I definitely would've tried it out on her. And then I suddenly remembered where I knew her from — we'd lived together years ago. She used to play the French horn for a local orchestra. That's how we met. I guess she was accusing me of having stolen her heart. Or maybe her life, though I know for a fact she took that with no help from me.

"You're up next," said the boyfriend again, still clutching his nose. His voice had a stuffed-up, trembly sound, and I thought with some satisfaction that maybe I had broken his nose. But between him nattering at me and my ex yelling at me, I thought maybe I had better get up there and do my part, though I wasn't quite sure yet what that was. Then as I climbed on stage, I thought almost nostalgically about the long walk I had taken that afternoon, the waters I had crossed, the rivers I had rowed, the streams I had pissed in my pants, the burnt and broken oar that made it all mean something, if only I could figure out what. I sidled up to my dancing partner as she launched the next verse of "Our Song", which sounded exactly like the two or three dozen she'd already launched, at least what I had been able to hear. I gave her a nudge to remind her I was up next, but she ignored me and kept on singing, so I launched my own bit on top of hers:

"You can't step in the same river twice," I shouted, "but you sure as hell can step in the same pile of shit. The difference is, the river keeps on flowing when you step in it, but the shit just sticks to your feet — "

I was about to continue in this vein when my dancing partner gave me a shove, and down below the boyfriend yelled, "You're missing the point!" But the audience broke into loud applause with cheers and whistles, and the band stopped playing and began taking bows. I guess they thought it was all for them, but I'm pretty sure it was mostly for me.

"I'm not done yet!" said my dancing partner. Her thick, dark eyebrows were drawn tight over her nose, and she looked furious, the first time I had seen her that mad.

"Baby, you were done before you started," I said. I shouldn't have said that, but I got carried away by all that applause.

"What did you call me?" she said, and swung her fist up against the side of my head. I had forgotten how strong she was and found myself flat on my back staring up at the sky. The ringing in my ears drowned out the applause. But the sky looked too much like ceiling tiles to be the sky, and the ringing in my ears was turning into a rhythmic beeping.

"We almost lost you there," said the woman in the bright, blue pants suit, except she wasn't dressed in a pants suit, she was wearing blue nursing scrubs. And I didn't think she was really talking to me, but only about me for the benefit of someone across from her. "But three whacks of defib brought you right back to us, didn't it, hon."

"Can he hear us?" said my dancing partner, her head poking into view.

"Maybe," said the nurse, "but we may never know how much he understands."

"Daddy?" said my dancing partner. "Daddy, can you hear me?"

"Gimme me a fucking break," I said, but she pretended not to hear me.

"It hardly matters," she said. Her head disappeared from view. "He never listened to us when he was up and around, I can't expect him to start now." Her head reappeared. "Daddy? I brought your granddaughter. Remember her, daddy?" Off to the side, barely in view, she held up the little kid I had met in the mall, the one who had asked me if I was a pervert. I couldn't see the kid all that well, so maybe it was the little man from the delivery service. Then I recognized the yellow tee shirt with the cute animal drawn on the chest. The kid didn't even look at me. She craned her head away as far as it would go and struggled to bury her face in her mother's shoulder. "I don't know why I expect him to recognize his own granddaughter, he barely realized she existed. He used to be an actor, so you'd think at least he could act the part."

"An actor?" said the nurse.

"Dinner theater. Except he made a commercial once. That was the high point of his career. Selling weed burners on late-night TV."

"Selling what?"

"Weed burners. Only $19.99 and you get two for the price of one if you order now."

"I could use one of those."

"Every time they ran that commercial he got a check. That's the only thing that kept us off welfare after mom killed herself."

"Two for the price of one? Really?"

"If you order now."

I groaned so loud it was almost a shout, but they pretended not to hear me. The voices drifted away, and I guess she and the nurse had moved to the far side of the room. I heard the low murmur of voices, but I couldn't make out the words, and soon a new voice joined in, a little louder than the others, the boyfriend's voice. He was asking something about amputating the rest of the arm, and my dancing partner was asking something about the risk, and the nurse said the doctor would be in soon, and their voices drifted away again. I guess the boyfriend was supposed to be my son-in-law.

But I know when I'm dreaming and when I'm not (even if I don't know how I know), and this had to be the weirdest dream of all. And that was about the meanest trick they'd played on me so far, whatever they were, whoever had cast that smarmy blowhard as my son-in-law. Maybe this was a dream within a dream. So all I had to do was close my eyes and wait for another dream to catch up with me. Or maybe close my eyes and wake up completely and not have to dream at all.

Then I heard a new voice, the kind man's voice, talking about pre-existing conditions, transient ischemia, blood clots, severe dehydration, cardiac arrest, and a number of other nasty-sounding words that couldn't have applied to me, because I'd be feeling fine if I could just get out of this fucking place.

The others listened in silence to the doctor kind man, till the boyfriend said, "It's a wonder the old man is still alive."

"I'm right here, asshole," I said. But they still pretended not to hear me.

Then for a long time I didn't hear anything, and I thought they had all left the room. But then I heard footsteps approaching, and the kind man doctor popped into view and smiled down at me. A speck of blood occupied the collar of his white coat.

"I know you can hear me, even if the others are not sure, so don't pretend you can't," he said.

"I know you can hear me," I shouted, "so don't *you* pretend you can't." And he kept on talking as if he couldn't.

"Here's what's going to happen," he said, and I wondered what movie I had heard that from. "You will awaken from a bad dream to the sound of pounding on your door, and only you will be able to hear it. Not your neighbor, not your neighbor's dog, but only you will hear that pounding on your door, and that's a door that only you can open..." He paused and grabbed my one good hand. "Here, let me help you up." In an instant I was standing and looking around at the crowd that had gathered. The band was still on stage. They were taking up their instruments again, getting ready for another rendition of "Our Song", I guess. "That was quite a fall you had," said the kind doctor man.

"What happened?"

"You fell off the stage. You must have got carried away with your performance, which was quite impassioned, I must say — ."

"I didn't fall off the stage, I was sucker-punched in the head." I looked around for my dancing partner, but I didn't see her anywhere.

"Memory plays tricks on you when you get carried away."

"So what about that pounding on my door?"

"What about it?"

"You were talking about that pounding on my door — what was that all about?"

"That pounding on your door? Must've been the pounding in your head."

"You said door."

"I'm pretty sure I just said head."

"No, you said door."

"I did say door, yes, just now, but first I said head."

"No, first you said door, then you said head."

On stage the drummer began working the bass drum with his foot. Maybe that was the pounding the man kind doctor was talking about. But I still think he said door. Or maybe he said head. Or maybe he said both. Or maybe he said nothing at all and I just imagined he had said something. I started to turn away from him, when suddenly he clapped his hand on his forehead.

"Of course," he said, "how stupid of me. It's your right hand returning to reclaim its owner. That's what's pounding on your door."

I'd had enough of this joker. He had once shown me some kindness the time he held opened the door when other doors had been locked against me, back when I would've been the one pounding on a door if he hadn't held it open for me. But I think by now he had exhausted my gratitude. I wanted to get away from him, but then he said, "And of course your question is the wrong question."

"About pounding on my door?"

"No. About how do you know you're not dreaming. There's no answer to that question. Of course, just because there's no answer doesn't mean you're not dreaming. It doesn't mean you are dreaming, either. It just means there's no answer — because it's the wrong question!"

"So what's the right question?"

"Now *that's* the right question."

If I still had half an oar I would've gladly pounded on his head with it, even though I didn't think that would've done much good. I shoved through the crowd, looking around for my dancing partner. Maybe she thought I was coming after her and decided to make herself scarce. But I don't think I was really coming after her. Or maybe I was, but only half-heartedly. More likely I was looking around to avoid her if I saw her.

I took a path out of the clearing. The band and its audience disappeared behind me and the noise suddenly died down when I lost sight of them. I couldn't hear anything, not even the wind in the trees. It was as if I had grown deaf again, like the time I had suddenly lost my hearing back when I came out of the causeway tunnel.

In fact, the shrubbery along the path formed a kind of tunnel, branches arching tightly overhead or whipping me in the face as I passed. I held up my good left arm for protection, and what was left of my right arm, and started running. I guess they really didn't want me to leave the park, whoever they were, or maybe they were just doing it out of pure meanness. I wouldn't put it past them. In fact, pure meanness explained a lot more than any well-thought-out plan.

In any case, the shrubbery was definitely trying to trap me, just like that dry thistle-thicket back whenever, and unfortunately this time I didn't have my weed burner with me. How's that for continuity? In a real dream I'm pretty sure that weed burner would've popped up out of nowhere just from my thinking about it. Unless I wasn't really thinking, but only dreaming I was thinking.

The branches were lashing my arms so hard, my arms started to bleed. I could hardly feel the pain in what was left of my right arm, but my left arm was stinging worse than when I had run into those stinging marsh weeds. I thought this time they'd finally caught up with me, whoever they were, or whatever, and they weren't going to let me go.

That suddenly made me so mad, I stopped in my tracks and grabbed one of the whip-lashing branches of a shrub and tore it off. It must've had thorns on it because it tore up my one good hand, which started bleeding a lot, but I didn't care. I was hoping the shrub would start screaming when I did that, like the trees in the forest I burned down, but it only shivered a little and sighed and grew still.

I wondered if the other shrubs would back off then, but they kept on lashing at me as I shoved on through the tunnel. I guess plant organisms in this park didn't really communicate with each other much, not as well as they did out in the country, anyway, so I had to keep tearing off branches as I pushed through them. That wasn't too easy with only one bloody hand, but eventually I made it through and found myself back on the street again, across from that restaurant with all the people eating lunch in it.

I didn't remember a park across from the restaurant last time I was here, so maybe it was a different restaurant, but it definitely looked like the same people inside were eating the same lunch.

Then I wondered if the restaurant and the band shell were one and the same thing, and if I had just circled back to where I had come from. Maybe I had fallen into an endless loop where everything was the same as everything else, and struggling from one place to another would always bring me back to the same place, no matter what. I crossed the street and got a closer look at the restaurant, and this time it definitely looked like a restaurant without the double image of a band shell, not like the last time I had looked at it.

Just then the delivery service truck pulled up in the street behind me, almost as if on schedule, although I'm not sure what that schedule was, or if there was a schedule. Maybe it was just some kind of stupid day-jaw-view. Maybe there wasn't a schedule and its arrival at that moment was just a coincidence, like everything else that happened this afternoon, if you can believe that. I'm pretty sure I can't.

I still couldn't hear anything and I hadn't heard the truck pulling up, but I saw it reflected in the restaurant window. I turned around as the little man jumped out and this time I was ready when he tossed the package at me. I caught it with one hand even before it hit the ground, and I shoved it right back in his face. The package was a lot lighter than when I first handled it. He caught it and threw it back at me and I batted it back at him and we volleyed it back and forth for a while, the little man getting madder and madder and screaming at me. I couldn't hear him screaming but his mouth was stretched wide open, lips writhing, tongue wagging, yellow tusks bared, and for once I was glad I couldn't hear anything.

Finally I got close enough to him I could smash the package straight down on his head. The package slid over his body and covered him almost to his feet. I guess my angry ex's ghost was no longer inside. Maybe she was still back at the band shell, and I hoped she was enjoying the performance. Maybe she could join the band. They would probably benefit from adding a French horn to the group. In any case, I had nothing against her so long as she stayed away from me, and I wished her the best. But maybe she was back inside the package and she and the little man were now squeezed in there together. They deserved each other.

He seemed to be struggling to get out, the way his feet were dancing and the box was reeling around on the pavement. I wondered why someone with teeth and jaws strong enough to bite through a steel chain would find it hard to bite through a flimsy cardboard box. But maybe it was harder being on the inside coming out than being on the outside going in, kind of like being in jail.

Suddenly I had an idea what OCCUPANT meant: not the occupant of my apartment but the occupant of the box. The box was addressed to its own contents, and had finally reached its destination. The thought made me laugh out loud, and deaf as I was I could actually hear the sound of my own laughter, though it seemed to come from a distance. In fact, the laughter seemed to go on and on even after I had stopped laughing, and I wondered whether that laughter was really mine. Or maybe there was more than one of us laughing. Though deaf as I was, I'm pretty sure it sounded like only one.

I kicked the little man out of the way and got in the truck, released the brake, put it in gear and took off. So what if I was driving a stolen vehicle? I was sure by now the cops wanted me for a lot more than that, and it definitely beat walking, biking or rowing.

In the side view mirror I saw the little man staggering around covered in the hatbox, or whatever it was, and I kind of hoped he would stagger out into the street and get run over. But I didn't see any other vehicles anywhere, not even parked vehicles. It must still be the street-cleaning hours. I didn't see any people, either. Maybe they were all in the restaurants eating lunch.

Except now I didn't see any restaurants, just one blank building after another, and I felt like I was driving through a ghost town. There are either too many people or there's nobody, and anybody you run into is never the one you want to meet. Maybe that's the biggest joke of all, what all the laughter is about. So tell me another one. Even if I don't get it I'll laugh, anyway, just to keep you telling more, whoever or whatever you are.

I almost felt like driving back to where I had left the little man in the hatbox. I wasn't sure I'd want to help him out of that box, though I was starting to feel kind of sorry for him and I guess I should've been grateful to him for getting me out of the police station, whatever his reasons were. But mostly I just wanted to stand in front of that restaurant and look in at normal people having lunch, just wanted to enjoy the pangs of my own hunger, the way normal people do during street-cleaning hours, a little past noon.

Then I wondered why street-cleaning hours happened during the lunch hour, a little past noon, when you'd think the streets would be most crowded, full of cars and busy, hungry people — and you should be cleaning your streets in the early morning hours when there's nobody around, shouldn't you, whoever or whatever you are that's running things in this town? So I didn't turn back. Those normal people having lunch, they were just a dinner-theater audience waiting for the show to start. Or maybe waiting for it to end. It's hard to tell when you only catch them in the middle of their lunch. So I kept on driving down, or up, that desolate, ghost-town street.

More time passed, I don't know how long, hours, days, centuries, before I noticed I was driving on fumes through open countryside. Not just open countryside, but a vast, brown, featureless plain that stretched in all directions to the horizon. I wondered if my dreaming brain had run out of ideas and it could only come up with a featureless plain. I mean, if it was really dreaming. If it wasn't, I don't know what I was looking at.

The motor died and the truck rolled to a stop. I pounded my one good bloody hand on the steering wheel, furious I hadn't been paying attention to the gas gauge. If I had noticed on time, I would've turned back before I ran out of gas. Well, since I ran out of gas, at least the laws of physics must still apply to the truck, so maybe I should stick to the truck, because who knows what weirdness was out there in that wilderness? So I should just wait here till something happened, the way it usually did.

But this time nothing did. My dancing partner didn't turn up unexpectedly, the boyfriend wasn't standing around jabbering at me, the school nurse (or whatever she was) wasn't grabbing at my necrotic arm, the kind man wasn't opening any doors for me, the little man from the delivery service wasn't misdelivering or re-misdelivering any unwanted packages.

I even would've welcomed my ex's ghost yelling at me in that great, blank wilderness. Or playing the French horn. That's how we met, after all. They had hired her to sit downstage-right and play French horn riffs. They had wanted an oboe player, but they only got her, and every time I shuffled on stage, she would play a single, long, low note on her horn. That note was the keynote of our early years together, a standing joke between us, one of those stories couples like to tell, How We First Met, and so on, ending in little loving snorts and giggles.

If I ever ran into her again I'd ask her why we thought the joke was so funny. Maybe the joke is what kept us together as long as we were. I don't know how long that was, but it must've been a long time if I can remember all this. If we could get back that joke, maybe now we could sit down in the dust and work things out. Maybe she could forgive me, or I could forgive her. Whatever it was that had to be forgiven. I'm not sure what. But I'm sure we could find something to forgive. Or at least make something up.

So I waited in the truck a long time, and when nothing happened I got out and walked to the rear, since — as the boyfriend once asked me back when he was a cop — how can anybody not do anything, even doing nothing is doing something? At least I think that's what he said. But maybe not. Or maybe it wasn't him that said it. I would've made notes if they hadn't taken away my pencil and manacled my hand.

I looked in the back. It was nearly empty but for three packages — a hatbox addressed to OCCUPANT and a couple of smaller packages addressed to normal people with regular addresses, though I forget what those were. Hatboxes had lost their charm for me, so I ignored this one, especially as I saw it wasn't addressed to me.

The others weren't addressed to me, either, but I felt a lot easier stealing from normal people than from someone who could've been anyone and even might've been living inside the package. The contents of the normal packages were disappointing. The first one I opened was empty, though I thought I heard it exhale as I opened it, as if it were heaving a great sigh of relief. So maybe it wasn't so normal after all. The second one contained a plain yellow scarf. I pocketed the scarf and got out of the rear of the truck.

I no longer thought it would make any difference which way I walked, so I just kept on in the direction the truck was pointing, straight ahead. I must've walked for days, and sometimes must've fallen exhausted in the dust, and maybe even fell asleep. Unless I was already asleep. But when I woke up (if I really did wake up), choking from all the dust that had covered me when I slept (if I really did sleep), it hardly seemed any time at all had passed. The sun still seemed to stand at a little past noon. The road had run out altogether, or maybe disappeared under that burnt-brown dust, which the wind blew endlessly back and forth across the plain, or piled up around my ankles whenever I stopped for a moment.

This time I kept the sun on my left as I walked, which I guess means I was heading north. Back then I had kept the sun on my right, so I must've been heading south after I had left home and started asking all those people downtown that stupid question. Which the little man from the delivery service had wisely called the dumbest thing he'd heard all day. I should've listened to him and stayed home.

In any case, south was not a place I wanted to revisit. I mean, if that's where I was coming from, and I'm guessing I was. So maybe keeping the sun beside my bloody but still good hand would get me to a better place than I got to back whenever. I don't know why I thought that. Ever hopeful, I guess.

I could mention I was crazy with hunger and thirst, but you already heard that story, haven't you, O you masters of the universe? And I don't want to bore you, if you aren't already, so I'm not going to tell that story again. Though you must know there's no such thing as boring, there's only bored, or if anything is boring it's only bored people, and I'm hoping you're not one of those, but if you are that's your problem, not mine.

And I could also mention I still didn't hear a thing, not the wind blowing in my ears, not the dust hissing across the ground. Except the sound of my own voice. I could hear that well enough, though it seemed to come from a distance. That's how I kept myself from getting bored. I started telling my own story, telling it out loud. Telling everything that had happened to me since I left home this afternoon, or whenever it was I had left home. I admit it's a hard story to tell, since I'm never sure where it happened, or when, or what the names of the characters are. Or even whether it happened to me. But if it didn't happen to me, whom did it happen to? Not being able to tell you that probably violates every rule of storytelling you ever heard of.

I still had that notebook and the fountain pen I pinched from the purse of my court-appointed psychologist. From time to time I stopped and jotted down some notes. I even wrote a comment about the difference between "who" and "whom", but I'm not going to include that in my story. I'm not trying to show you I know more about telling stories than you think I do. And you probably think that talking to you like this violates another rule. Like a dinner-theater actor stepping out of character, off the stage, and sitting down to share a meal with someone in the audience.

I'd hate it if someone did that to me while I was eating. Hungry as I was, I was in no mood to share a meal with anyone. But I will share my story with you.

Then the wind began to pick up. Dust whipped around me, filled my shoes, drenched my hair, rose into the sky, blotted out the horizon, dimmed the sun, and soon earth and sky were the same burnt-brown color of dust. I took out the yellow scarf and wrapped it around the lower half of my face. Thanks for leaving me that, whatever you are, whoever's in charge of the weather around here. I'd like to believe you did it out of kindness, but by now I'm pretty sure you're a sadistic psychopath who likes to prolong suffering. But what if I decided I'd had enough, what if I just lay down in the dust and closed my eyes and refused to go any farther? Bring it on, assholes, do your worst.

But I didn't lie down, not just yet. Every step I took — and the step after that — and the step after the step after that — I told myself I'd take one more step, and then maybe I'd lie down. But that thought led to others. Maybe I really was back there lying in a hospital bed, surrounded by family impatiently waiting for me to die. And that voice I heard from a distance, that wasn't my voice telling my story, that was someone sitting beside the bed, reading to me.

But that didn't make much sense. Nobody would be reading that kind of story to me. Everyone I knew could hardly read. And those that could, hated it. And nobody I knew had enough imagination to make up such a story. I don't know how I knew that, since I don't remember knowing anyone all that well. Just flashing back on the past again, I guess. But I'm pretty sure this is *my* story, anyway, this is what happened to me.

By now I was walking with my eyes closed. The wind had probably blown me off course, but that hardly mattered, since I couldn't see anything, anyway. I just let the wind push me from behind in any direction it wanted. Until finally I did lie down, deciding I wasn't getting up again. A little later the wind stopped blowing.

The sun came out and I felt its warmth on my face. I guess you must've got bored just watching me lie in the dust, so you had to provide a little encouragement, but I just lay there with my eyes closed, feeling the warmth of the sun on my face, and the calm, cool air, waiting for what you had next for me. I tried to imagine what it would be. How about another flood? Fine, let me drown. But make sure it's real water this time. Maybe you'll send another rowboat to rescue me, but you'll never get me to climb aboard. How about a fire? I hadn't seen anything combustible out here, but I'm sure you'll come up with something, so let me burn. How about an army of fire ants crawling all over me? Ravening wolf packs, flesh-eating flowers? I already feel half eaten up, so you might as well finish the job. Let the world freeze over, let the earth open up beneath me spitting fire and brimstone, let the sky fall, I'm ready for it.

I soon ran out of disasters to think of, and none of them happened. That's the last thing I thought of: that absolutely nothing more would happen again, ever. That was the scariest thought of all. I sat up and opened my eyes, just to make something happen.

And just then it came to me that maybe I was the only one making anything happen. Maybe that's what they've been telling me all along. Of course I wondered what it all meant. How could I not wonder that? How could anybody? I bet even you're wondering it, whoever, whatever you are. And how could anything mean anything if I'm the only one making anything happen? How much sense does that make?

I was sitting on the curb of a sidewalk, my feet in the gutter. Somewhere I must've lost the yellow scarf. I looked down at the ground between my feet. I looked up and down the street, or down and up the street, and it all seemed familiar to me.

Just then the rest of my right arm fell off at the shoulder and snaked along the gutter and disappeared around the corner. I hardly paid attention to it. But maybe I was a little surprised it had stayed attached this long.

I raised my left hand. "This is one hand," I said to it. "There are no others." Somehow I found the thought comforting, trivial as it was. I wondered when the next piece of me would fall off. I wondered which piece it would be. Probably my shoulder. Then all of me, piece by piece. But I wasn't going to worry about it. It felt good just to sit down after such a tiring day.

The day had turned chilly. Winter must be setting in. That would be the second time this afternoon. Maybe this time for real. In the east a bright, full moon had appeared. Wispy clouds hovered around it. The moon would be bright enough tonight to cast a whole kennel of moon dogs on its halo.

I looked west and thought the sun had moved a considerable distance since the last time I checked it. It seemed to be moving faster to the west than I had ever thought possible. I couldn't look at it directly, but the shadow it cast was getting longer by the second. As if it had to make up for a lot of lost time. Soon the sun would set, but I knew my apartment building was not far off, and I was no longer in a hurry to get back. I'd be home before dinner, crack open a beer, maybe two beers, probably three or four beers, and microwave a frozen dinner. I'd put on some music, listen for that beautiful note I heard back at the farm. It would coddle me, reassure me, heal me, grow me a new arm, make me whole again. If nothing else could, that would. That beautiful, long, low note.

It felt good just to sit in the dimming sunlight. I even began to feel sleepy. But then I worried about that, because a sleepy man can't be sleeping, and so he can't be dreaming. If I was feeling sleepy, I must be awake. But maybe a sleepy man can dream wide awake. Maybe that's what I was doing. Dreaming wide awake.

If I was only dreaming, I would soon wake up, or maybe wake up even more if I was already awake. I don't know why I was waking up so late in the day. I guess I was never an early riser. In any case all would be resolved in a moment and vanish in a puff. I would wake up and laugh and say, What a stupid dream. I would beat up my sleeping brains for entertaining such stupid dreams. Till then I just had to be patient.

Anyway, I was alive, I still had my hunger and thirst and the pain in my left arm to prove I was still alive. Maybe my left arm would fall off, too, and take the pain with it but I almost hoped the pain would stay. For the first time I began to appreciate that fact. If all my limbs fell off and my body disintegrated I would still want my appetites, still want to feel my pain, because I was sure the dead can't have appetites or feel pain. Even if they were hungry ghosts, their hunger would give them some kind of life, because their hunger is also ours, and that's why they haunt us, that's why they live.

I still had that notebook and fountain pen, so I decided to finish writing down everything that had happened to me this afternoon. I was afraid I would run out of ink, but I never did. And I didn't think that shabby little notebook had enough pages for me to write down everything, but I seemed to have filled hundreds of those pages. I don't know how I could've written so much in the short time I've been sitting here, trying to keep the notebook balanced on my knee while holding it down with my bloody left hand, which had never been my writing hand.

In fact, most of the pages are filled with an illegible scrawl which I'm unable to read, like everything else I've written or tried to read this afternoon. The words are sometimes vaguely familiar, but every time I think I've made out their meaning, they change their shape and seem to mean something else. But maybe that's just the way words are.

But at least the time has passed quickly as I sit here resting up for the last leg of my long walk home, which can't be more than half a block down the street, or up the street, whichever it is, if memory serves. But maybe it doesn't. Maybe it's neither up nor down the street, but I'm always hopeful. That's what dreams are for, after all, hopeful delusions like our stories, even the bad dreams, because you can always hope to wake up from them, and every dream, like every story, like time itself, must have a stop when you finally wake up into a world from which there is no waking up.

So maybe I should just stay sitting here. It's not so bad here, and I'm always hopeful. I wouldn't have come this far if I hadn't been hopeful. I would've stretched myself out in the wilderness and cried myself to death. Like I almost did back in the dusty, dirt-brown desert. Or maybe I'd be back in that hospital, or whatever it was, listening to all their bullshit while they pretended not to hear me, trying to bullshit me to death like everyone else I met this afternoon. But they didn't succeed, nobody did, because I stayed hopeful and kept on walking.

I heard someone approaching and looked up. He seemed vaguely familiar. For some reason I thought he was someone who might know the answer to my questions. I nodded at him, but he stared straight ahead, pretending he didn't see me, and he walked on by without speaking.

## About the Author

Jon McKenney is the author of a previous novel, *Fust*.

www.ingramcontent.com/pod-product-compliance
Lightning Source LLC
Chambersburg PA
CBHW071258130626
46556CB00003B/1374